A CASTLE COURT CHRISTMAS

A REGENCY CHRISTMAS ANTHOLOGY

HALEY MARIE   CHLOE K. JAMES   MADISON BAILEY

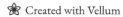 Created with Vellum

CONTENTS

ETERNALLY YOURS
Haley Marie

HOW TO LOSE A MATCH IN
10 DAYS
Chloe K. James

A CHRISTMAS PROPOSAL
Madison Bailey

ETERNALLY YOURS

HALEY MARIE

CHAPTER 1

"Gwendolyn, are you prepared to depart?"

Gwendolyn despised the question from her mother. She sighed, "No..."

This dreaded moment had been sinking into Gwendolyn's heart since her father, Mr. Lockhart's passing in the weeks prior. When her father had become ill with consumption, it was unknown where the inheritances he left behind would turn to. Her father had no living brothers and no sons to which his home would transfer to through succession. Before he passed, Mr. Lockhart mentioned the possibility of having a male cousin who the home could transfer to. However, per the rules of society, this would mean that Gwendolyn and her mother and sisters would not be able to continue to reside there.

How cruel a world this was.

After her father had passed, Mrs. Lockhart wrote to this aforementioned cousin, who to their surprise, replied. Though he offered his sincere condolences, he took ownership of the home and provided the remaining Lockhart's a quaint residence in the nearby town of Castle Combe.

Though Gwendolyn adored Castle Combe with its simplicity and picturesque features, losing her childhood home broke her spirits. The home was built by her father, and he was a very imaginative man. He built the home with hidden spaces, an attic, and an unruly garden. All of which made home to many childhood games and mischief between Gwendolyn and her two younger sisters, Annette and Clara.

As Gwendolyn solemnly stared out of her bedroom window, she felt the warmth of her mother's hand on her shoulder. "I understand you, my dear. However, this is our reality. We have been blessed to have Mr. Atwell be generous enough to secure a new home for us. We should be grateful."

"It would be more generous if he were to simply allow us to continue living here. It is *our* home. We had never heard of this man's existence until father became ill. A shame he has the right to claim what is rightfully ours." Gwendolyn stated in annoyance.

Mrs. Lockhart gave an exhausted sigh, "We simply need to remember to be grateful."

Deep in her heart, Gwendolyn knew her mother was right. This was the reality of her world, and there was nothing that she could do to change that. She was forced into acceptance, but she would not do so in a graceful manner.

Gwendolyn decided she would leave a note for Mr. Atwell. She wondered if she were able to get him to sympathize with her family, she would have a chance to secure her home back.

Gwendolyn walked into her father's study and lifted a newly sharpened quill off of the desk. She dipped it quickly in the ink beside her, and began...

"I HAVE SECURED a residence for you, my friend."

Hugh Beaumont removed the smoking pipe from his

mouth and curiously looked at his friend. "What do you mean, Cornelius?"

Cornelius Atwell was sitting in his large armchair, his pinpoint nose buried deep in parchment papers. "A distant cousin of mine has passed. He leaves a home which will need ownership. Certainly, Mrs. Atwell and I have no need for it."

Hugh removed his pipe again, releasing a puff of smoke. "Are there no heirs to leave the home to?"

Cornelius shook his head, nose still buried in the parchment. "I am the closest family he has. Poor man."

Hugh continued to look curiously at his friend, "There were no other heirs to claim ownership? No children?" Though Cornelius Atwell was a great friend, he often left his responses dense and lacking pertinent information.

Cornelius chuckled, laying the parchment in his lap as he looked at Hugh. "Of course the man had children. But, they are all women."

Hugh grew concerned, "What is to be of these women being left behind?"

Cornelius lifted the parchment back up to cover his face. "Be not concerned, my friend. I have secured them a comfortable residence."

"Very generous of you. Though, I am still curious as to why you are transferring their home to me." Hugh placed his pipe back in the corner of his mouth, "I cannot reside in a home which is not rightfully mine."

Cornelius frustratingly dropped his parchment-filled hands into his lap and looked at Hugh, "What am I to do with it, then? I am in no need of a second home and you lost your means of obtaining a home at all." Hugh looked down at his lap and held his pipe nervously. He knew Cornelius did not mean to offend, he was an honest man, even sometimes brutally so. "Accept what I am giving you," started Cornelius in a reassuring tone, "Perceive it as a new beginning."

Cornelius lifted the papers once more to read. Hugh continued to face away from his friend. This act of generosity was the most kindness Hugh had experienced in months. Mostly, Cornelius was correct. Hugh no longer had the means to obtain any home at this state in his life. Those opportunities had been lost and left in his past. This would be a new beginning for Hugh.

CHAPTER 2

Hugh stood, staring at the front door of "his" new home. The door reminded him of his own home. It had been made of the same material, a natural oak. Hugh had a flashback of when he left his home, turning to look at the door one more time as it was shut in front of him. Hugh winced. He reached toward the brass knob, but paused for a moment and pondered if he should knock or simply enter. Of course, knocking before entering an empty home seemed humorous, but this home did not feel like his own.

Hugh reached for the knob again and sighed, "To a new beginning" he said to himself.

As he entered the home, the must smell of an empty home filled Hugh's nostrils. There was a chill to the home that was somehow colder than the late November chill outside. Hugh placed his portmanteau in front of the door to prop it open, allowing the early Winter air to breathe through the musk.

Hugh walked farther into the home and looked around to see the surrounding rooms on the first floor. He found the dining parlor, kitchen, and drawing room occupied on the first floor. As he looked into each room, he was surprised to find that there was quite an array of furniture and decorum had been left behind. Hugh was relieved to find this, now he would not have to find those things on his own or ask Cornelius to pay for them.

As he made his way through each room, he pulled off the large sheets that covered the furniture and tossed them to the side. As he did so, dust flew through the air. He waved his hand in front of his face in an attempt to prevent himself from breathing in the dust. The furniture was an older style, but again, it reminded him of his previous home.

Once he had explored the main floor, he made his way up the staircase to find this floor contained three bedrooms and the study. Within the wall, next to the study, he noticed a small cutout. It was almost invisible with how well it had blended in. Hugh walked closer to the wall and saw the carved images of flowers covering the entire area. Hugh tried to push against the cutout, but there was no movement. He felt around for any type of knob or handle, but had no luck.

Hugh went into the study, tossing the sheets to the side again. As he uncovered the desk, an unusual sound was made, the sound of a crumpled paper flew past his ears. Curious at the noise, Hugh looked around the floor. As he moved his foot, he noticed a folded piece of paper beneath his shoe.

He picked up the paper and noticed it had been addressed to Cornelius. Hugh could clearly see that the handwriting was a woman's. From the previous residents, no doubt. Hugh placed the letter back on the desk, but quickly looked back at it.

Normally, Hugh would not open a letter addressed to someone else. However, he wondered if the note contained instructions for the home. His curiosity got the best of him, and he picked the letter up again.

" Since the very unfortunate and most distressing passing of my father, I knew that this home would no longer remain in our keeping. I must admit, I was quite hopeful that since my father had no living brothers or sons, that the home could stay with us. Imagine our surprise when we learnt of your existence! How gracious you were to remove us from our present home to somewhere unfamiliar."

Hugh knew that these were most certainly not sincere words of gratitude.

"I anticipate that you will enjoy this home very much, as we have enjoyed it as our only home these many years. You should know, my father built this home with his own hands, which is why this place holds so dear to my heart."

There was that tone, again.

Hugh read about the secret areas, the gardens, the paintings. He looked up to glance around the room and noticed a painting to his right. The painting depicted a beautiful, wild garden. In the middle of the garden was a small, white bench. Well, not perfectly white. The painting had incredible detail to show that the bench was well-worn and weathered. The bench was covered in vines, ivy and roses. Exquisite detail.

Reading about the attic is what peaked Hugh's interest the most.

"Of course, despite all of these memories being shared, I understand that you are likely to improve this home with many fine decorations and adjustments. You may even take it upon yourself to keep our garden. Though the thought of this saddens me greatly, it seems that it is no longer my concern."

There was that tone, again. This woman was certainly not happy about this arrangement. Hugh was relieved that he was the one who had come upon this letter, and not Cornelius. It was then Hugh felt a pull in his heart. Hugh realized that he and this mysterious author had something in common. Both had lost someone they loved, lost their inheritance, their homes, their comfort. Hugh understood her pain.

"Miss Gwendolyn Lockhart," Hugh read as his eyes revealed the mystery author's name.

Hugh folded up the letter again and placed it back on the desk. He was not sure what to do with it. He was unsure giving it to Cornelius was a good idea, as Miss Lockhart was clearly upset with him and Cornelius would most likely misinterpret her letter and write back expressing how pleased he was to have appeased the family. That scenario would certainly make matters worse.

Hugh thought about writing to Miss Lockhart, himself. He thought about telling her his newfound appreciation for the home after reading her letter, in hopes this would bring her some comfort. However, he was not sure how to address it. Surely, it was not appropriate for two seemingly unmarried strangers to write to one another. There was also a chance, if Hugh was to use his real identity, that she would know of him. The Beaumont name was quite popular among good society. Rumors of Hugh losing his inheritance had surely made its way through the mouths and ears of all good society.

Hugh decided that he would write Miss Lockhart one letter, under the name of Cornelius Atwell. It would only be one letter to help ease some of this young woman's pain, who had lost almost equal to what Hugh had lost.

What conceivable mishap could ensue?

CHAPTER 3

"So, how does the home suit you?" Cornelius asked as he shoveled a spoonful of boiled potatoes into his mouth.

"It suits me fine," replied Hugh as he watched Cornelius with a small bit of disgust.

"Oh, good. How fortunate everything has worked out." replied Cornelius.

Hugh nodded, though he desperately wanted to ask his friend about Miss Gwendolyn Lockhart. However, Hugh knew that Cornelius was unlikely to know much specific details about her. So, he kept his next question simple.

"Have you heard how your late-cousins family are doing?"

Cornelius wiped his mouth with his napkin and placed it beside him "I assume well enough."

"You have not inquired?" asked Hugh.

Cornelius shook his head and took a swig of his drink, "I do not believe I have a need to, do you believe otherwise?"

"I simply wonder if they might take pleasure in hearing from you. After all, you are family." suggested Hugh.

"I am certain they are quite comfortable. You are familiar

with my previous summer home in Castle Combe, are you not?" asked Cornelius.

Hugh looked up from his plate, Castle Combe was a place he knew very well. "Ah, yes. Is that where they are residing?"

Cornelius nodded.

Hugh tried to cover a smile with his napkin. Hugh was *very* familiar with the small town on its own, and he knew where Cornelius's summer home resided. He had spent time there over numerous summers when Cornelius was still a bachelor. Now he knew where to send his return letter.

"Your kitchen has filled me yet again, friend. That was the most splendid supper." complimented Hugh.

Cornelius nodded in agreement. Not looking up from his plate as he continued to eat.

Hugh excused himself and headed for the front door.

"Hugh," Cornelius rushed out of the dining room, "Join me next week. Same day and time."

Hugh smiled as he turned back to his old friend, "Of course."

They shook hands and Hugh walked out of the front door, entering Cornelius's carriage to leave.

As soon as Hugh entered through his front door, he rushed to the study and shoved his quill into ink, splattering the page.

Dear Miss Lockhart,

I was very surprised when I found your letter, and I am very grateful I did. I am sorry to hear that you are so upset about your displacement. However, I truly believe that you will come to find yourself quite comfortable in Castle Combe. I have many fond memories of that quaint little town, and I believe it is the perfect place for a new beginning.

Tell your sister that her paintings are remarkable. I have never seen such talented art. I have not been able to enjoy the gardens quite yet, as the beginning of the winter freeze has taken effect. I am excited to see how it flourishes in the Spring. I make a promise now, to not attend any of your beloved gardens.

I must also tell you that I have tried many times to find that access to your secret attic. However, I have had no luck.

I have much enjoyed your home.

Best wishes,

Mr. Atwell

Hugh sealed the letter and placed it down at his desk. He gave a deep sigh, trying to calm the anticipation he had been feeling. He stared at the letter, he hoped the remnants or even the arrival of his letter, would not offend Miss Lockhart.

"This will only be one time and is only to ease her mind," thought Hugh.

Now, another dilemma. Hugh was unsure of how he was going to go about sending his letters to Miss Lockhart. He had no personal staff of his own, or the money to hire personal staff. He thought about delivering the letters himself, but that would not be possible once the Winter started to settle in.

Hugh then thought of using Cornelius's staff. He was dining there every week, so it seemed a much more reasonable option.

CHAPTER 4

G wendolyn was very stunned as she gazed upon the envelope in her hands. It was addressed to her, written in an unfamiliar handwriting.

It had to be from *him*. Mr. Atwell. Maybe her plan had worked. She ripped open the envelope and quickly scoured through its contents.

As she finished the letter, she sighed. Her plan had not worked. There were hints of pity toward her, but Mr. Atwell was clearly more interested in the home itself *because* of her letter as opposed to giving it back.

"What is the matter, dear?" Mrs. Lockhart asked as she saw Gwendolyn's face turn to disappointment.

Gwendolyn looked up at her mother, "He wrote back. The dreaded man had the nerve." Mrs. Lockhart said nothing as she looked at Gwendolyn in pure confusion. Gwendolyn continued, "I left Mr. Atwell a letter in father's study. I told him of our fond memories of them, in hopes that he would take pity on us and give back what is rightfully ours. Alas, my plan was a failure. He seems to have taken more of an interest in our home now." She tossed the letter on the table and exhaustedly dropped down in the chair next to her. Mrs. Lockhart slowly reached out for the letter, pulling it towards her to read it.

"Hmm. I see your predicament." Mrs. Lockhart started, "I am sorry your plan did not work. However, attempting to trick a man into gifting an entire *home* is...well...quite a complex feat."

Gwendolyn plopped her chin in her hand and gave a frustrated response, "He could. If he truly felt sorry for what he had done, he could have done it."

Her mother shook her head, "I do not believe it is that easy, my dear. Though, he does state that Castle Combe is the perfect place for a new beginning. That sounds most reassuring!"

Gwendolyn scowled. The words "new beginning" echoing in her mind. She did not need, nor did she want a new beginning. She was happy with the life she had. Before the loss of her father, her home, her sanctuary. She had been forced into this new beginning.

"Are you going to write him back?" Annette had asked from the other side of the room, seemingly she had eavesdropped on Gwendolyn's conversation with her mother.

"I do not know if I want to heed his advice." replied Gwendolyn.

"Well, my dear," started Mrs. Lockhart, "He seemed to have taken interest in whatever you told him." she then smirked. Gwendolyn rolled her eyes.

FOR A REASON UNBEKNOWNST TO HUGH, he had felt very inspired to visit Castle Combe today. He could not figure out why, but the small town was somehow calling to him.

After some thought, Hugh figured he could benefit well from a new set of quills and parchment.

In the weeks since Hugh had sent his letter to Miss Lockhart, Cornelius had been kind enough to purchase a horse for Hugh. He was lovingly named *Corny-boy* after his old friend. Hugh found the horse to be a bit stubborn at first, but it gave Hugh a challenge, and Hugh liked challenges.

The ride into Castle Combe was calm and quiet. Snow flurries gently floated through the air around him. Hugh found this to be most relaxing.

When Hugh entered Castle Combe, it was just as he had remembered. The bustling crowds and snow-covered cobblestone. Hugh smiled as he looked around him. Just as he had always remembered.

Hugh found the quill and parchment shop and stepped inside to gather the items he needed. As he walked out of the shop, a great gust of wind shot a large object towards Hugh, which whacked him on the forehead.

"Gah! Ouch!"

Hugh ripped the object off of his face. In his hands he noticed a deep-red bonnet with a blue ribbon tied around.

"Oh my! Sir! I am so sorry! Are you alright?"

Hugh looked up at the voice in front of him and froze.

She was beautiful. Breathtaking, even. She had light blonde hair, that *had* been done up, until the wind had seemingly started to loosen the curls from their pins. Blonde curls framed her small pale face. However, Hugh's focus could only be kept on her pale blue eyes.

"Sir...?"

Hugh cleared his throat, "Apologies, miss. I am quite alright, only startled." Hugh followed her eyes as she looked up towards Hugh's forehead. The expression on her beautiful face changed from embarrassment to grotesque. Hugh lifted his finger to his forehead, it felt cold to the touch. As he brought his finger down to view it, he noticed the blood.

"Ah, just a small flesh wound." Hugh teased.

The young woman started to quickly rummage through her handbag and pulled out a handkerchief, handing it to Hugh. "Please, I insist."

Hugh grimaced , "You may not want it returned."

She shook her head, "I will make another, please."

Hugh reluctantly took the handkerchief and placed it on his forehead. He put his tophat on his head to hold the handkerchief.

"Might I have my bonnet returned, sir? I promise to never allow the wind to take it ever again."

Hugh laughed, "Ah, yes. Of course." He nervously held his hand out with the bonnet, "I trust you will keep your promise?"

The young woman laughed. Hugh's stomach felt light.

"Yes, I shall. Thank you for being so understanding." She curtsied to Hugh then quickly turned on her heel and walked away.

As Hugh was making his way home, he realized he had forgotten to pick up more necessities. "Blast it!" he shouted. Not only had he forgotten more supplies, he had also forgotten to ask for the woman's name. Hugh often prided himself on being more flirtatious, but this young woman had caught him completely caught off-guard. He thought of her pale blue eyes. He had never seen a shade like that in his life. He thought of her light blonde curls framing her face, he thought of her laugh. His stomach began to feel light again.

When Hugh returned home, he put Corny-boy into the stall for the night and made his way inside the home. It was getting dark, Hugh made his way into his bedchamber and lit a candle. He lifted his candle and made his way to the other side of his room to view his wound in the mirror. He lifted off his tophat, and the handkerchief fell to the table. The cut was not in horrible condition, it had already seemed to start to heal. Hugh looked down at the handkerchief and picked it up. As he grabbed it, his thumb grazed over embroidered thread. He paused.

"Her initials!"

He looked at his hand that was holding the handkerchief and moved it closer to the flame, but made sure not to get too close. He certainly did not want to damage it. As he looked closer at the embroidery, Hugh could not believe his eyes.

Only a coincidence, surely.

Hugh's heart was pounding. There was only one way to find out if what he thought could be the truth. He would have to return to Castle Combe.

"G.L"

CHAPTER 5

Hugh made certain to travel to Castle Combe the following day. To obtain the rest of his needs, of course. While roaming throughout the freshly snow-covered cobblestone streets, he found himself entering shops he had no need to be in. Hugh could not help but look around at each face near him. In doing so, he noticed two young children, brothers perhaps, throwing small snowballs at one another. They were having such a grand time, until an older woman scolded them from a nearby shop.

Hugh smiled, it reminded him of when he and his brother, Matthew would come to Castle Combe as children. They would play in the streets, causing a ruckus as brothers often do, and get scolded by either their mother or an older woman. Whoever saw them first.

Hugh's mother had been raised in Castle Combe. Visiting this small town with his mother and Matthew was one of Hugh's fondest childhood memories. This town could make you come alive, especially in the winter. Being surrounded by cheerful neighbors, wassailers, snow covered streets and shops, made you feel comfortable. Castle Combe felt like home.

Hugh acquired the rest of the items he was in need of and made his way back home. Once he arrived, Hugh found a letter on the front steps. He hurried to put Corny-boy away and once inside, broke the red-crested seal.

Dear Mr. Atwell,

I must admit something to you. I did not want to give this town any opportunity upon moving here. I was upset with you, with how you had displaced us. I was hoping in your reading of my letter, you would take pity on my family and give us our home back. I apologize for having ill-intentions with that letter. My mother, being the wise woman that she is, has since convinced me to give this town a chance. I have been doing so, and I must say, I was happily surprised. This quaint, little town has much more than I thought. I believe that, in time, I could grow to appreciate Castle Combe.

In regards to the garden, I thank you for not having the desire to maintain it at this time. I believe, if you give it an opportunity, you will find it to be most relaxing once all of the many flowers start to blossom in the Spring.

As much as I would like to give you guidance in finding our secret attic, I am afraid it may take all of the fun from you.

Seeing as I have not been very kind to you already, I should show kindness now and neglect to give you further information on the matter.

However, I do wish you luck.
Sincerely,
Miss Lockhart

Hugh grinned. She was challenging him. He quickly made his way to the study to craft a response.

Dear Miss Lockhart,

Your mother is a wise woman, indeed. I have many fond memories of Castle Combe from my youth, and I still find it quite pleasant to visit even still. As Christmastide is drawing near, and I must state that you are incredibly lucky to be witness to the magic that is Castle Combe in Christmastime, I hope you will enjoy the beauty and comfort of your surroundings. Castle Combe truly comes together around this time of year, it is impossible to feel alone.

I must admit something as well, I was greatly looking forward to you sharing more clues as to how I could find this "secret attic". However, I do enjoy a challenge, so I accept yours. I noticed a small door-shape near the study, the wall carvings are incredible. I am *certain your father is to credit for that.*

Anyhow, I am curious if that would be a good place to start my efforts.

You need not comment on my previous statement. I simply thought that information might be interesting to share.

Sincerely,

Mr. Atwell.

P.S. Have you become acquainted with anyone interesting now that you are embracing Castle Combe?

A few weeks passed since Hugh sent his latest letter to Miss Lockhart. A freeze started to chill the air, snowfall becoming heavier each morning. This made it quite challenging for Hugh's fine steed to desire to tread into town or ride to Cornelius's home. Hugh found it challenging for him as well, and though he enjoyed challenges, snow was not one in which he fancied.

With more time to occupy himself, Hugh spent more time exploring inside the home. He tried to find any nuances that he could share with Miss Lockhart. Especially if those nuances led him closer to solving how to access the attic.

Hugh also spent more time reading. Many books had been leftover in the study. He found these books to be both interesting and insightful. There was a vast array of subjects to choose from. History, Politics, Geography, Sciences, Arts, Poetry, and Music. It was obvious to Hugh that the late-Mr. Lockhart was a very well-rounded and well-educated gentleman. He assumed his daughters would have possibly followed suit.

A few days later, as Hugh was exiting through his front door to go feed Corny-boy, his foot made a *crunch* noise as he stepped. Due to the snow, Hugh would not have thought much about the sound, except it was louder than usual. He looked down and realized there was an envelope underneath his foot. Hugh quickly picked up the envelope and went inside to the study, where he had just lit a fire. He put the envelope close to dry it out, he hoped that it was not too late.

Once the paper seemed dry enough, Hugh broke open the seal. The words were slightly smeared, but Hugh could still make out what they said. He was grateful his newfound pen-friend had exquisite handwriting.

Dear Mr. Atwell,

I have shared your kind compliment to my mother, and she wanted me to tell you that she appreciated that greatly. She would also like to thank you for the home you have provided us.

Hugh's heart sank when reading that last sentence. A reminder that he had been lying to Miss Lockhart.

As the snow starts to fall here in Castle Combe, I am beginning to sense the charming comfort you so described. The amount of wassailing is a bit much for my liking, but I can not deny that it does bring a sense of cheer. More neighbors and acquaintances at church have started to invite us to more parties and tea times, so it is true what you say, about feeling lonely here. I believe we will not feel so during this Christmas season. My mother and sisters need that, desperately.

My sister has had the pleasure of becoming acquainted with a group of young women from the church who share her gift of painting. She is able to socialize with them each week as well as further develop her talent. Mother has also met some women at church who have included her into their friendship. These women are widows themselves, and they often spend their days sharing stories of their husbands and children, which can be quite humorous. I have appreciated these women greatly, for my mother has been able to laugh again because of them. I believe they have helped soften her grief. They have softened mine as well.

I do not socialize much. There are a few neighborhood women who I occasionally have tea with. However, most of my socializing is with you.

Hugh's heart jumped.

To answer your previous question about having experienced a curious encounter, I must admit that I have!

Around a month ago, my family and I were strolling through Castle Combe. As we were walking between shops, a large gust of wind blew my bonnet off of my head! I had mistakenly forgot to tie it around my chin earlier that day. A mistake I will surely never make, again.

Hugh wondered if what Miss Lockhart was talking about could be what he thought she could be.

Well, the wind blew my bonnet with such force, that it hit a gentleman on the head and he bled!

Hugh paused and reminded his body to breathe.

Oh, Mr. Atwell. How mortified I was! I offered my handkerchief to the gentleman in an attempt to mend what had happened. What made it worse, and I shall only admit this to you because we are family...

Hugh's heart stung.

...the gentleman was quite dashing.

Hugh's eyes widened and his heart jumped. This was confirmation that the breathtakingly beautiful young woman whose handkerchief he still possessed, was indeed Miss Gwendolyn Lockhart!

It is only my own sheer luck that something this humiliating would happen to me. I am grateful however, because I have not seen this man since and I am hoping it will stay that way.

Regarding your comment about the mysterious door-shape you have found near the study. That is quite a curious discovery you have made, but I will add no more to that subject.

Hugh mischievously grinned.

Miss Lockhart

P.S. I would greatly appreciate hearing your fond memories of Castle Combe, if you feel so inclined to share.

CHAPTER 6

Hugh read the letter over and over and over again. He could not help himself from the excitement in knowing that he had met Miss Lockhart, and she was an equal in both her wit and appearance. He liked her.

Just as quickly as the excitement had entered him, it became replaced by guilt. He could not confess to her now. Not after she had revealed her attraction towards him. That would not be the act of a gentleman, to humiliate her like that. Hugh also knew that if she were to find out, she would no longer write to him, he was most certain. He would go back to being alone in the world, aside from Cornelius, of course. The thought depressed him greatly.

His thoughts moved from Miss Lockhart to his brother, Matthew. He thought back to their last encounter...

"Hugh. What have you done?"

Matthew's face lay in his hands. Exhaustion emanated from his demeanor like a foul stench.

Hugh was speechless. There was no excuse that he could give.

Matthew moved his hands from his face and he slouched back in his armchair, his arms crossed in anger.

"Do you have anything to say about this?"

"...It...It was a rigged game, Matthew. I did not realize..."

Matthew slammed his hands on the desk.

"You do not know anything! Our parents are dead and all you care to do is gamble away!"

Hugh frantically shook his head, "It was a moment of weakness, Matthew. I never intend to do it again."

Matthew scoffed, "Only a moment? You mean to lie to me now? I know you have been gambling since we lost our mother and you have been hiding it. How could you allow yourself to get into this situation?"

In truth, Hugh was quite meticulous when placing bets and was always successful in not gambling his money away in games. Winning was a habit for him. Second nature, even. Hugh had a talent for reading other men's "tells". Matthew was right, too. Hugh had started gambling after their mother had passed. It was Hugh's way to distract himself from the pain.

"Give me a loan, Matthew. I will make this up to you. I will find a good means of income and repay my inheritance, with an interest." Hugh begged.

Matthew shook his head, "There is no accommodation I could give you and no means of income to replace what you have lost."

Hugh knew Matthew was referring to his trust. It was lost now.

"Matthew, I beg of you. Nothing of this sort will happen again."

Matthew huffed, "I am not giving you a loan, Hugh. You

are on your own. You must grow up, and learn to live with the consequences of your actions."

Hugh found it hard to catch his breath, trying to hold back the tears that were now filling his eyes, "That leaves me nothing. What am I to do..."

Matthew held his hand up to interrupt Hugh, "You should have thought of these consequences before you gambled for the first time. I wish you luck, truly." Matthew then turned his chair around to face the fire and sat down. His back was now facing Hugh. Hugh knew what this meant. His father would do the same actions when he was cross with someone.

As Hugh was leaving his home the next day, he walked past a portrait of his mother that hung in the main hall. It was her most recent portrait before she passed. He looked into her large, brown eyes. Begging for them to look back at him. Begging for them to let him stay.

GUILT WAS an emotion that was all too familiar to Hugh. Somehow he kept placing himself in situations that nearly consumed him.

To clear his mind, he made his way to the study. He stopped in front of the doorway, looking to his left. It was easier to make out the odd door shape now, but he had no idea how he was to open it. It certainly would not push open. He had tried that all too much. He walked toward the hidden door, running his hands along the carvings that blended into the wall. No knob, nothing to insinuate how the door would open.

Hugh was unsure how he was going to figure it out, but for Gwendolyn, he was happy to take on the challenge. He was determined to find some way to open this mysterious entrance. He just needed some hint, some clue as to how.

Until he was given a better idea, he wrote to Miss Lockhart.

Dear Miss Lockhart,

I would be delighted to share some stories of my time at Castle Combe. My mother was born in Castle Combe and spent her entire childhood there. She adored it. The small town made for many close friendships between the townspeople, as well as a comfort to call the town home. My mother always spoke about how Christmastime was her favorite season to celebrate because of Castle Combe. As a young boy, that confused me. I could not understand how a town could make Christmas better than it already was.

Once my brother and I were older, my mother took us there over Christmastime to experience Castle Combe. The moment our carriage entered the town, we saw it in all its glory and celebration. I then understood, even as a small child, how Christmas became more exciting there. It soon became a tradition to visit Castle Combe each year. As my brother and I grew and were able to travel on our own, we continued that tradition.

Unfortunately, since my mother has passed, I have not been able to convince myself to visit the town again. The memories seem to be too painful for me. However, I am happy to know that your family is beginning to thrive there. I am grateful the town is still the same, friendly, pleasant place as I remember it to be.

Regarding your story on the dashing young man, I must agree that you have the most unfortunate form of luck. I am grateful I did not have to witness such an embarrassment. Though, I am disappointed I was not privy to it.

I must thank you for the variety of books left here. They have entertained me greatly.

Sincerely,

Mr. Atwell

CHAPTER 7

G wendolyn found herself feeling excitement when Mr. Atwell's letter came. She found comfort in his letters. She looked forward to their arrival. A man who seemed like the enemy had turned into a friend, a friend she needed.

"Gwennie, what are you smiling about?" asked Mrs. Lockhart.

Gwendolyn waved her hand in the air, as to insinuate to her mother that it was nothing of much importance, "I received another letter from Mr. Atwell. His mother was from Castle Combe, supposedly. She would bring Mr. Atwell and his brother here frequently as children. Seems as though those are some of his fondest memories."

Mrs. Lockhart grinned, "That is lovely to hear. I am glad to see you are becoming great acquaintances with Mr. Atwell. I do believe this new friendship is good for you."

Gwendolyn looked up at her mother, she thought of how angry she had been to be displaced to Castle Combe. Thinking of the loss of her father and home brought her great sadness, but she was starting to find peace. Mr. Atwell had brought that peace for her.

Hugh was having his weekly supper at Mr. Atwell's home. Conversation was basic and dull, until Cornelius made a statement that greatly surprised Hugh.

"We will be hosting a Christmas ball this year." stated Cornelius with seemingly no enthusiasm.

Hugh's head shot up from looking at his plate, "Ah, that sounds like a splendid idea. People love a good Christmas celebration. When shall it be held?"

"Well, we were thinking of hosting soon. Beginning of December should suffice," replied Cornelius.

Hugh thought for a moment, "I see. Usually a Christmas ball is held on Christmas day."

Cornelius paused from eating, fork mid-air, "Oh. I believe you have a point. However, we are meant to be staying with Mrs. Atwell's family during that time. Should I reconsider?"

Hugh knew how socially important this ball would be to his friend, "Oh no, my friend! A Christmas ball celebrated early will be just the thing to help get everyone in the holiday spirit. I believe it is most splendid and practical."Cornelius grinned and continued eating, anything that was practical was most pleasing to him.

"Mrs. Atwell must be excited, is she not?" asked Hugh, though he already knew the answer.

Cornelius sighed and glanced toward the dining hall entrance, seemingly checking to see if Mrs. Atwell was returning from feeding their new infant. "Yes, she is. That is her personality. She is more sociable than I."

Hugh was not certain how to respond to Cornelius's statement. It was true, Cornelius was not a sociable person. Which was not an unfavorable trait to Hugh, but unfortunately it was to those in High Society.

"Do you know who you will invite?" Hugh asked.

Cornelius nodded as he chewed, "Ah, yes. Mrs. Atwell has provided a lengthy list of families she would like to attend. No one that I am necessarily familiar with. Except for you, of course. Oh! And my late-cousins family will be invited, the Lockhart's."

Hugh choked on the food he had just attempted to swallow.

"Good gracious! Are you quite alright?" Cornelius asked with great concern.

Hugh frantically guzzled his drink and took a deep breath, "Ye-yes. Sorry. The food seemed to have another route it desired to travel."

"I dare say." agreed Cornelius, "Anyhow, the invitations have already been sent."

Hugh did not know what else to say. He was still trying to recover from his choking mishap and was trying to calm his nerves about Gwendolyn being in presence soon. Cornelius went on to talk about other subjects that had no relation to the upcoming ball, but all Hugh could think of was how he was going to handle the impending situation.

Hugh wanted to write to Miss Lockhart and tell her the truth of his identity, but the lie had been carried on for too far at this point. Surely, if she knew the truth, she would be too upset to continue any type of correspondence. This had to end, but it had to end innocently.

After much thought during Cornelius's random ramblings, Hugh came up with a plan. This plan was simple. He would end his correspondence with Miss Lockhart, giving the reason for having to focus on his new child or another reasonable reason. Then, they could meet at the ball in an organic manner and he could attempt to court her in an honest way.

Hugh grinned. His plan was perfect.

CHAPTER 8

The evening of the Christmas ball had arrived.

Hugh stood outside as Cornelius's carriage arrived at Hugh's front step. He was filled with anxiety. Since Hugh was made known about the ball, Miss Lockhart had written to him twice. He had read these letters, but had not written her back. The first letter she had sent to him had been sent before her knowledge of the ball, at least, that is what Hugh assumed as she did not mention it. Miss Lockhart had thanked "Mr. Atwell" for sharing his memories of his late-mother. In return, she shared memories of her father. Mr. Lockhart was a man who dearly adored his daughters and wife. He often referred to his daughters as his roses. This made sense to Hugh as to why he had preferred his garden unkempt. Miss Lockhart had attempted to be discreet in inquiring with him if he was able to find their secret attic, but Hugh had not been occupied in searching for it since his supper with Cornelius.

Her next letter then contained her excitement for the ball. She expressed her anticipation in meeting "Mr. Atwell" and how she was looking forward to being able to finally thank him for all he had done for her family and for her. When

Hugh first read this, he felt ill. He pondered telling Cornelius that he had become sick and would no longer be able to attend, but he knew his presence was far too important to his friend to concoct an illness that Hugh did not feel.

All Hugh needed to do was figure out which excuse to use to end the correspondence, which he would worry about at a later time and hope that Mr Atwell, being as unsociable as he was, would not keep himself around to speak with any party guests. Tonight, his goal was to meet Miss Lockhart for the "first time".

The carriage stopped abruptly. Hugh peered his head out of the window and saw that he had already arrived at Cornelius's home. Many party-goers had already arrived at the residence. Hugh could hear the laughter and music echoing outside. The knots in Hugh's stomach had made their way up to his throat.

The carriage door opened and Hugh took a deep breath as he placed his tophat upon his head and exited. The front doors swung open and the echoing of laughter and music had turned into roars. Relief warmed over Hugh's anxiety as we walked in and noticed the amount of people. Surely, there was no way Mr. Atwell and Miss Lockhart would be able to find one another in a manor this full.

As soon as Hugh had that thought, he felt the presence of someone standing so closely behind him, that their breath was tickling the back of Hugh's neck. Hugh turned and jumped at the sight of Cornelius. Their noses nearly touching.

"Hello Cornelius...Your ball has turned out most exquisite..." said Hugh as he took a few steps back.

"Yes, Mrs. Atwell has surely out-done herself. She is enjoying it greatly," responded Cornelius frankly. A trickle of sweat dripped from his forehead.

"As she should be." Hugh grinned.

"*Monsieur Beaumont!*" Hugh could recognize the clearly

false French accent anywhere, he turned to see Mrs. Atwell making her way toward him and Mr. Atwell. Her face was flush and red from having just danced in the ballroom.

Hugh curtsied, "Mrs. Atwell. A most splendid ball you and Mr. Atwell have accomplished. You have such talent."

Mrs. Atwell blushed and covered her face with her fan, "*Oh, merci, Monsieur Beaumont.* You really should not make a married woman blush, so."

Hugh laughed nervously and looked at Cornelius, hoping that his friend would say something in response. Mrs. Atwell was much more extravagant than Hugh preferred. Cornelius said nothing as he stared at his wife.

Mrs. Atwell then grasped at Cornelius's arm and yanked him towards her, nearly making the large man fall on her, "*Mon chérie*, we should go dance among our guests!"

Cornelius' face had somehow become whiter than it already was. He had opened his mouth in an attempt to speak, but he was too stunned.

"Let me have the honor, Mrs. Atwell!" Hugh loudly insisted, regretting it instantly.

Mrs. Atwell let out an obnoxious gasp, "*Avec plaisir, Monsieur Beaumont!* I do love dancing. It is a shame my dear husband does not enjoy it so."

Hugh extended his bent arm to Mrs. Atwell, and the two walked together into the ballroom. As they entered and found a place in the dance line, the musicians started to play an old English country dance. Throughout the dance, Mrs. Atwell continuously shifted her focus to the others around her, socializing as she danced. Hugh kept his focus on the dance steps, trying to avoid causing any attention to himself.

Partway during the dance, the couples sashayed opposite each other, which caused everyone to switch partners for a brief moment. As Hugh grasped the hand of another young woman and turned to face who his new partner was, he instantly made eye contact with a pair of pale blue eyes.

Eyes that were all too familiar.

Hugh froze. Miss Lockhart froze as well.

It was not until Mrs. Atwell spoke up that the couple both realized they were not dancing along with the others, "*Monsieur Beaumont*, you must dance with your partner!"

Hugh shook his head and grasped Miss Lockhart's hand again to dance.

WHAT SHEER LUCK SHE HAD. Gwendolyn could not believe that her new dance partner was none other than the handsome gentleman who had worn her bonnet on his face. His deep sea eyes staring straight into hers.

Thankfully, a boisterous woman had spoken up to help the two of them come back to reality. Gwendolyn did her best to keep her eyes off of the young gentleman. She was afraid to look at him and possibly blush, or even worse, there was a chance he could remember who she was.

They sashayed away from each other and were back with their original partners. The dance then finished. When Gwendolyn came up from her curtsy, she looked toward the young gentleman and regretted it instantly. He was looking right back at her. Gwendolyn immediately shot her gaze down to her shoes. He had to have remembered her by now.

Gwendolyn exited the ballroom to find her mother speaking with the boisterous woman from the ballroom and a large, tall gentleman. As she approached them, she heard her mother say, "We thank you kindly for all you have done for us, Mr. Atwell. Castle Combe has proven to be the most lovely place."

Gwendolyn smiled. Her friend and confidant was

standing before her. He was not who she expected, though. He was quiet and did not make much eye contact.

"Of course."

Gwendolyn then spoke up, "Mr. Atwell." she curtsied, "I am Miss Lockhart, whom you have been writing too. It is so lovely to finally meet you in person. Now I can formally thank you for your kind correspondence that has helped ease my pain during these difficult times."

Mrs. Atwell shot a confused look to Mr. Atwell who also gave that same look to Gwendolyn. Gwendolyn's stomach sank. Something was not right.

"I have not written to anyone." Mr. Atwell said and he shaked his head.

In fear of what Mr. Atwell had just stated, Gwendolyn protested, "Mr. Atwell, please. We have been writing since late-November. Surely you must be teasing me."

Mrs. Atwell then spoke up, "Mr. Atwell does not take part in "teasing". Believe me. You are quite mistaken in whom you have been writing. *Cependant*, we are glad that you have been enjoying Castle Combe! We have only been there but a few times, right *mon chérie*?"

Mr. Atwell gave no response but a nod. Gwendolyn's heart began to race. Her face flushed.

Mrs. Lockhart gently placed her hand on Gwendolyn's arm, "I have been witness to these letters. Surely, somebody from our home has been writing to her under your name, perhaps?"

Mrs. Lockhart's question sparked a realization in Gwendolyn. She had wondered why the location of the ball was not the same as her previous home. Now it made sense, someone else was living in the home. *Her* home.

"Mr. Atwell," Gwendolyn started, "Who has been occupying the home these past few months?"

Mrs. Atwell responded again, "Oh! Why, Mr. Atwell's

meilleur ami. His name is Mr. Beaumont. Quite a dashing young man...Oh! Miss Lockhart, he had been your other dance partner in the ballroom!"

Gwendolyn had been right. He did know who she was. "Of course," said Gwendolyn to herself. Her initials had been embroidered on the handkerchief she had given him after the dreaded bonnet incident. The letters. The lies. Gwendolyn's face became hot, her mind started to feel as if it was rushing. She pulled out her fan and started to fan herself at a heavy pace.

"Pardon me, I need some air." Gwendolyn said breathlessly as she bolted up the set of stairs next to her. She ran into the nearest room at the top, which happened to be the Atwell's drawing room. She slammed the door behind her.

She closed her eyes and turned around, resting against the door. As she opened her eyes, she noticed a gentleman was in the room with her. He was standing in front of the window, but he was looking at her. It was *him*.

CHAPTER 9

G wendolyn took a deep breath in and turned to attempt to leave the room, calmly.

"Wait!"

Gwendolyn remained turned away from Mr. Beaumont, her hand holding the doorknob.

"I...did not...well, was unable to...um...introduce myself earlier..."

Gwendolyn was appalled by the nerve he had in this moment. She interrupted, "There is no need for introductions...Mr. Beaumont."

SHE FIGURED IT OUT.

Hugh's worst fear had happened. The guilt became all too consuming. "You deserve an apology..."

Miss Lockhart spun around and interrupted again, pointing her finger at him, "I should say so! You take my childhood home from me, are dishonest about your identity, then have the nerve to "introduce" yourself now!"

41

Hugh held his hands up, as an attempt to block himself from her words, "It was not malicious, I insist. I was planning to share the truth..."

"When?" Miss Lockhart shouted, "After you allow me to embarrass myself to you regarding our first interaction? After you allowed me to share my emotions about the loss of my father? After you completely settle your bearings in *my* home?"

Hugh continued to hold his hands up, "It was not my choice to occupy your home, Miss Lockhart..."

"No, but you received the luxury of my losses!" Miss Lockhart was screaming now. Tears had started to stream down her perfectly pink cheeks.

Hugh lowered his hands, shaking his head, "No. There is no luxury in a loss such as yours. I sympathize with your emotions."

Miss Lockhart scoffed, "What reason should I have to believe you? I have been nothing but a game to you."

"No!" Hugh rejected, "You have not been a game. When I read your first letter, I felt for you because I share your pain. I thought, perhaps, I could help you..."

Miss Lockhart shook her head.

"I understand why you do not believe me now. But, you must. Every word of those letters was true. My memories, my enjoyment of your home, all are mine. I did not fabricate anything more than a name." Hugh begged.

Before he could say anything more, Miss Lockhart flung the drawing room door open and left, slamming it shut behind her.

A WEEK HAD PASSED since the Christmas ball. Mrs. Lockhart had already received an invitation from Mrs. Atwell to come and dine with them on that current night. Gwendolyn did not desire to go, the pain of the revelations from the ball still lay heavy on her heart. Much to her dismay, her mother insisted it was for their best interest. A "new beginning", she had referred to it.

Gwendolyn deeply resented that term. It reminded her of Mr. Beaumont. A memory that had once brought her joy, now brought her pain.

When they had arrived at the Atwell's residence, Gwendolyn immediately noticed the additional amount of Christmas decorum that Mrs. Atwell had added into the home. Even more than had been displayed the week prior. She greeted Mr. and Mrs. Atwell as she should, seated herself as she should, and enjoyed her meal as she should. Throughout the evening, Gwendolyn found that she quite enjoyed Mr. Atwell more than she expected that she would. He was very straightforward and honest with his responses, Gwendolyn appreciated that.

After dinner, they went into the dining room. Gwendolyn could not stop thinking about the disaster that had occurred in that room. Her sister began to play the pianoforte, Gwendolyn sat next to Mr. Atwell. She assumed that he was not likely to speak much to her, and that she could enjoy her sister's playing in silence.

She was wrong, of course.

"I am sorry about your home."

Gwendolyn looked at Mr. Atwell in surprise, "Thank you, Mr. Atwell."

Mr. Atwell spoke again, "I am a logical man, Miss Lockhart. Thinking with emotion is not something I am good at. When I inherited your home after your father's passing, I was not thinking about your family's feelings. I had no use for your home, and Mr. Beaumont did. It made sense for me to give it to him.:

Gwendolyn nodded. Seeing it from Mr. Atwell's perspective made some sense to her. "Might you tell me a little more about your friend? Even though I was seemingly writing to him, I feel as if I do not know him at all."

Mr. Atwell sighed, "Not many people care to be my friend, Miss Lockhart. However, Hugh...Mr. Beaumont, does. He has always been good to me. After the death of his mother, it was incredibly hard on him. Then following the loss of his father, he became worse."

"Hugh" thought Gwendolyn, she liked his first name. She recalled Hugh's statement about understanding her pain. "What do you mean when you say he became worse?" she asked.

Mr. Atwell replied, "When Mr. Beaumont's mother died, he turned to gambling. He became quite skilled in those silly card games. One night he got into trouble playing a rigged game and he lost his entire inheritance."

Gwendolyn could not speak. She did not know what to say.

Mr. Atwell continued, "He went to ask his brother for more money, but Matthew said he had to start a new life without it"

"That is why you gave him the home." Gwendolyn interrupted. Mr. Atwell nodded.

Gwendolyn chuckled lightly, "Mr. Atwell, you have contradicted yourself. You said that you are not talented at thinking with emotion, however, you gave my home to your friend when he was in need. You are an emotional thinker, Mr. Atwell, and a very fine one."

Mr. Atwell smiled at Gwendolyn, she smiled in return.

"Mr. Beaumont told me that he grew up in Castle Combe, that his mother had taken him there many times as a child. Do you know that to be true?" Gwendolyn asked.

Mr. Atwell nodded, "Very true. His mother is from Castle Combe. It is a large reason I secured a home there for your family. Mr. Beaumont always spoke about how much he liked the little town. I thought another family would enjoy it, too."

Gwendolyn smiled, "You are very correct, Cousin. Another fine example of what a wonderful emotional thinker you are."

Mr. Atwell smiled at Gwendolyn again, "Your company pleases me, Miss Lockhart."

Gwendolyn smiled and held her glass up to toast with Mr. Atwell, "Your company pleases me as well, Mr. Atwell."

ANOTHER WEEK HAD PASSED since the dinner at the Atwell's. Gwendolyn's thoughts still frequently drifted to the ball. She thought of their fight and felt great remorse. After learning of his backstory from Mr. Atwell, the anger and pain that Gwendolyn had felt against him had changed to forgiveness.

Christmastime was strong in Castle Combe. Walking the cobblestone streets filled with wassailers and children playing in the snow made Gwendolyn fall in love with the town. She found that she started looking forward to church, tea with neighbors, and walking around the town. He now understood why Hugh's mother would bring her children here often.

There was a connection in Castle Combe, now. A happiness.

As the days passed, Gwendolyn began to re-read her letters exchanged with Hugh. She began to miss his letters, she began to miss *him*.

Knowing what she knew now about him, she felt awful about what she had said in anger. The accusations she made against him. She pondered writing to him to apologize, but Hugh had every reason to be angry and hurt with her. Surely, he would burn any letter sent.

Little did she know, more than a letter would soon come her way.

CHAPTER 10

Two weeks had passed since the Christmas ball, but for Hugh it felt as though only it was only yesterday. He had to admit to himself that he felt a sense of relief now that Miss Lockhart knew the truth, but knowing he had lost her pained him greatly.

In these last weeks since he and Miss Lockhart's quarrel, Hugh had come to the conclusion that he needed closure of the main pain in his life. He decided to write to Matthew.

Dear Matthew,

I hope this letter finds you well.

Cornelius Atwell, who I am certain you remember, has been so kind as to give me a home at no expense. I only care for it. For him to entrust me with such a large responsibility has been frightful, though I believe it is also in my best interest. In fact, there is quite an interesting story to it, if you would care to hear in the future.

There are no other residents in this home other than I. Oh, and a horse. Another gift from Cornelius. I have lovingly named him "Corny-boy" in his honor. I have been tempted to keep him in the house with me to ease my loneliness, but the thought of horse dung retching the house and only I alone to clean it changes my mind rather quickly. I have been alone in this home, with only my thoughts and memories. Which is why I write to you now.

I miss you terribly, brother. I want to offer you my most sincere apologies. Since my departure, I have been consumed with guilt for the consequence of my addictions. Know that I harbor no ill feelings toward you. In fact, I applaud you for doing what was best for me. I know, as well as you I am certain, that had you given me more money that I would have lost it to my addictions. I have not stopped thinking of our parents either, mother mostly.

I have actually found myself in another predicament. Due to my own actions, of course. Cornelius received my current home from the loss of his cousin. His cousin had no male heirs, so naturally they went to Cornelius and he moved them to Castle Combe. When I first moved into the house, I found a letter from one of the daughters. She was so distraught at the losses she had endured. I felt for her. I understood her. I wanted to help ease her pain, but I did so under Cornelius's name. Foolish, I know.

Little did I realize that in attempting to help her, she was helping me. I have fallen for her, Matthew. The lie came to light at a recent ball a few weeks ago and I have surely lost her forever. Losing her has reminded me of losing you, and though I am certain that I shall never correspond with Miss Lockhart again, I am hopeful I might receive a reply from you.

Wishing you the best,
Hugh

Christmas day had approached. Hugh had yet to hear from Matthew. He tried his best to occupy his time so we would not become stuck in his own thoughts. He attempted to find that attic once and for all.

He stared at the flower carvings on the wall. All different kinds. He did not know how he was going to figure it out. He had tried the books, nothing stuck out in his mind from what he had read. It was certainly some sort of puzzle. He wondered if the garden could contain a clue, however the grounds were completely buried in ice and snow. If there was a clue residing on the grounds, Hugh would not be able to know where to start.

Hugh started to feel the stings of disappointment. Suddenly, there was a knock on the door. Hugh ran down to find a letter on the floor inside. It had been pushed between the door and doorframe. He lifted up the letter to the light, assuming it would be from Cornelius.

It was from Matthew.

Hugh,

I am beyond pleased to hear that Cornelius has taken you under his wing. He was always my favorite friend of yours.

Your letter has found me most shaken. I was certain that the day you departed would be the last day I would see you. Though I appreciate your apology, I would like to apologize. In my anger with you, I did not extend grace. I knew you were not your addictions, yet treated you as if you were. For that, I am dreadfully sorry.

I accept your apology, should you accept mine.

I am most anxious to hear more about Miss Lockhart. I should also tell you that I believe not all is lost. If you were able to have hope in finding peace with me, I express that you should make that same attempt of hope to Miss Lockhart.

Speaking of meeting young women, I am married now. You remember Miss Rose Stonewall, our neighbor...

Hugh stopped reading Matthew's letter at this point, "Rose...of course!"

Matthew's new wife sparked a memory in Hugh. Mr. Lockhart referred to his daughters as his "rose", a rose had to be the key to enter the attic.

With Matthew's letter in hand, Hugh ran back up to the wall, searching for a rose. He knew he found the opening the moment he saw it. Three roses planted beside each other with a lily in between. Each rose for a daughter and a lily for Mrs. Lockhart, no doubt. Hugh placed his empty hand on the carving and found it was loose, like a doorknob. He twisted it to the left, and the door made a loud "thud" as it opened. Dust flew off of the wall.

Hugh opened the door more and saw a steep set of stairs. He quickly went into the study to place Matthew's letter down and light a candle. Once that was done, he made his way up the attic steps. Upon entering the attic, there was a slight chill. It was dark, with only the light of a tiny window to give any light. Though to some, the room would be the least bit comforting, Hugh understood why Miss Lockhart was fond of it. It was tranquil.

Sunlight peered through the small window onto a large square object on the other side of the room. Hugh went closer and turned the square over.

It was a painting. A painting of a house, signed by Mr. Lockhart.

Hugh smiled and shook his head while he laughed. With this newfound peace and closure from Matthew, now it was time for Hugh's heart to find peace once again.

GWENDOLYN WAS SURPRISED to hear her mother call her down that afternoon, for they had already had their exchange of gifts that Christmas morning. Gwendolyn came down the stairs and made her way into the drawing room. Immediately upon entering, she froze.

Hugh Beaumont was standing in the room, holding a large canvas that she could only see the back of.

Gwendolyn debated internally whether she wanted to embrace Hugh or cry out an apology.

"I found the attic." started Hugh. Gwendolyn gave no response. Hugh continued, "I have so much to explain to you, and so much to apologize for."

Gwendolyn spoke up, "There is no explanation to be had, Mr. Beaumont. Mr. Atwell explained your situation to me a few weeks back. I was very rude to you during our quarrel and I need to apologize to you for that."

"You deserve to have an explanation of everything, at least" replied Hugh.

Gwendolyn nodded, ready to hear what Hugh had to say.

Hugh talked about the loss of his parents, how that led him into a gambling addiction, how he lost his inheritance. He talked about his last encounter with Matthew, he talked about finding her letter and understanding her. He explained how he was too afraid to use his own name and why, and how foolish he was for doing so.

Hugh then made a statement that made Gwendolyn nearly melt, "In the attempt to help ease your pain, you have eased mine. You allowed me, encouraged me, to open up to you. To trust you. When I realized that I had encountered you in town that day, or your bonnet, rather. I was bewitched. Then at the ball..." Hugh sighed, "I care deeply for you, Miss

Lockhart. I should have given you my trust from the beginning and been honest with you."

Gwendolyn smiled softly, if only he knew how she had come to feel something for him over this past month.

"What is in your hand, Mr. Beaumont?" asked Gwendolyn.

Hugh turned the canvas around. Tears immediately filled Gwendolyn's eyes, she covered her mouth with her hands. She had not seen her father's painting in years.

"There is more..." started Hugh, "I have reconciled with my brother. He is going to help me attempt to secure a new home. Therefore, I have no need to reside in yours any longer..."

Gwendolyn quickly sat herself down.

"I have spoken to the real Mr. Atwell. The home is yours, again." Hugh grinned.

The tears that had filled Gwendolyn's eyes now streamed down her cheeks. She stood up and ran to Hugh, embracing him. He returned her embrace with pleasure.

"Merry Christmas, Miss Lockhart." he whispered, softly.

"Gwendolyn." she replied. Hugh smiled.

Hugh was so warm, so kind. She did not want to part from him and he seemed to not want to part from her. She held onto him until she felt Hugh begin to pull away. She looked up, Hugh moved his hand to cup her cheek, wiping a tear away with his thumb.

"Your eyes. They are the first image that comes to mind when you enter my thoughts."

Gwendolyn blushed, "Though your eyes are just as beautiful, I cannot say they are the first image that comes to my mind when I think of you."

Hugh looked at her curiously, "What is the first image that comes to your mind, dare I ask?"

"My bonnet." Gwendolyn teased.

The two roared with laughter. Hugh, with his hand still holding Gwendolyn's cheek, pulled her face closer to his.

They paused for a moment, but this time Hugh did not need a remark from Mrs. Atwell to tell him what to do next.

My dearest Hugh,

I am pleased to hear the home is being well kept as this Winter turns to Spring. Please continue to keep a watchful eye on that barn, it has been many years since my father built it and I worry he will get wet inside as the snow melts. If he starts to complain of the moisture, he must become a house pet. Which would be rather unfortunate for us.

I am also pleased to hear that Matthew is to be staying with you before the wedding. I am filled with excitement to finally meet him and hear more about your childhood together.

My mother is most pleased with our upcoming arrangement. She will enjoy remaining in Castle Combe with my sisters and you and I tend to our home.

Regarding your previous question, I do not believe it is silly that we still continue to write to each other. For through our letters is how we came to know each other.

I hope you will continue to write to me, always.

Eternally yours,
Gwendolyn Lockhart

P.S. You are still not allowed to tend to our garden come Spring.

ABOUT THE AUTHOR

Haley is a mother, wife, nurse, and now an author. She enjoys spending time with her family, playing board games, and reading many different genres. She is currently working on a historical nonfiction of one of her pioneer ancestors and will be releasing a Regency romance soon! Look for her next book, Helen Clarke, coming early 2024.

 instagram.com/h.b.reads

HOW TO LOSE A MATCH IN 10 DAYS

CHLOE K. JAMES

ALSO BY CHLOE K. JAMES

Deceiving Mister Thornton

Beneath the Sycamore

CHAPTER 1

Day One

9 Days Before Christmas Day
Castle Combe, Wiltshire County, England

W hy Benjamin Blackburn was standing in my drawing room at this present moment, I could not fathom. Not only could I not fathom it, but I also despised the reason; even though I did not quite know why. There was no possible way that Mr. Blackburn would be in *my* home for anything good. The last time he had been in my house, the tyrant had also brought in a toad and mortified the wits out of me for refusing to kiss it.

At the time, I had been eight and I had absolutely no idea how to kiss, but even now, ten years past, toad kissing was not a journey that sounded intriguing enough to embark on. When that torment came to an end, I shoved him out and told him never to call on me again. Since then I had been in earnest to keep him out of my house and I had been successful.

Alas, until today.

My mother, father, and the six of seven siblings that did not deserve to be addressed by name, even surrounded him.

I faked a smile. "My, Mr. Blackburn. What an honour to see you today. Why are you here?" I did not intend to sound impolite, but for heaven's sake, it was *him.*

It was not Mr. Blackburn who replied, but my father. "Anna, Mr. Blackburn and I have come to an arrangement." And to Mr. Blackburn, my father nodded.

Mr. Blackburn came ahead and knelt in front of me.

Oh dear.

Even though I was not listening to him, as my mind was a jumbled mess of asking myself *why* and desperately craving a biscuit, I still knew what he asked. I responded as so: "I would rather roll in mud and dung like the pigs outside."

It seemed, however, that I had no choice in the matter and, not before informing me that the engagement would be announced at the Christmas Day ball, my father sent me to my bed-chamber as penance for acting like a heathen in the presence of company. I would miss supper, yet Mr. Blackburn would stay.

To my misfortune, I was now engaged to be married to a man whom I despised because, most likely, he needed a wife and I was undecidedly available and therefore chosen to fulfil the absurd task.

This plan would need to be put to an end and it would not be difficult to obtain, as I'd always been bright and quick-witted.

Castle Combe was home to me, not only because I had lived there all my life, but because Molly Rabbitt, my darling friend, lived near enough that we were able to communicate with one another from our bed-chamber windows. Molly seldom spent time out of her bed-chamber since she had already secured a man. A *bore* of a man to say the least. So boring, in fact, that it was humbling, for I was the exact opposite. Molly became my dearest friend and my confidante two years prior, just after she had gotten married.

While it was not likely that my father expected me to say in my bed-chamber any longer, I was angry at him for securing my engagement to Benjamin Blackburn of all men, so I would not be leaving it until I came up with a plan.

I wrote a note explaining my quandary, then tied it to a rock and signalled to Molly with my lantern for her to open her window. My signal caught her attention immediately and she obeyed. Before tossing the rock, I showed it to her as a warning and she nodded, implying that she would catch it.

Her flowerpot was broken, but all in the name of friendship.

The plan that Molly assisting me in coming up with by dint of tossing the aforementioned rock back and forth through each other's window with notes tied to it goes as follows: I was to convince Mr. Blackburn that he very much *did not* wish to proceed with this marriage. My first act of tomfoolery would be performed this very night.

I did not like the way that I caught my breath when I re-entered the drawing room several hours after that terrible proposal because Mr. Blackburn had grown into his mole quite well. I also hated the way that my hunger made itself known in such earnestness; it might have been humbler in its endeavours. My family, along with myself, tensed. However, I heard Mr. Blackburn snort in the silence. I mentally retracted my pig comment from earlier, for if *he* was going to be a pig as well, then I would be some other creature far away from the likes of him.

"Miss Appleton," he greeted warmly. *Grotesque.*

Now was my opportunity. Molly had always praised me for pretending to enjoy her husband's company when I came around to spend time with Molly; he was truly too dull for his own good. "Oh, Mr. Blackburn!" I wailed and fell to the floor, flipping my hair to cover my face. "Oh, Mr. Blackburn, I am wounded by my words this afternoon and I apologise for wounding you!" I then crawled to where he sat and flipped my hair back to its rightful state (I had convincing tears at this point). "I panicked, for I have dreamt of you all my life! Will you please, please, *please* forgive me?"

My family looked pleasantly horrified and Mr. Blackburn sat in frozen confusion, blinking in silence as he considered what had just happened. "All's well that ends well, Miss Appleton. You are forgiven." He finished with a grin, though I could not believe it to be a genuine grin seeing as his mouth twitched.

Unless that meant that he was trying not to laugh.

"Call me Benjamin. We are to be married, yes?" His grin was without a doubt, genuine.

Grotesque, indeed.

In less than a fortnight, he would undoubtedly want to turn back.

CHAPTER 2

Day Two
8 Days Before Christmas Day

As I finished the painting, I wished that I might have procured a plan to get Molly out of her own engagement to her husband. However, I found that I was a bit too late for that. She'd have succeeded greatly, poor thing. I wiped my finger off on the cloth near me and held the large canvas out in front of me, smiling. Usually, I was a much better artist, but this would do for reaching today's goal. Most artists would have most definitely considered finger-painting a waste of perfectly good canvas, but not I; *not* using it for this reason was a waste of brilliant potential.

Benjamin sat in the drawing room of my home with father, Benjamin's close gambling friends, Tobias Bradley and Theodore Lewis, and a man named Reginald. I supposed those three gentlemen were to be part of the wedding that would not take place with the knowledge that my plan would not end with a veil falling down my blonde curls.

I checked the time. Molly should have come knocking on the front door two minutes ago.

I groaned quietly enough that the men did not hear me and I turned on my heel back upstairs to my bed-chamber. When I arrived up there, I saw through my window that Molly had *barely* walked out her door to move forward with our plan. Lovely. In approximately thirty seconds, a knock sounded on the door. Without a servant to open the door, my father paused the conversation in the drawing room and opened the door himself where, with a grand swiftness, Molly began to ramble about her injured knee.

I heard her tell my father that she had slipped on ice, to which he responded that she could not have slipped because it had been snowing all day. Meanwhile, Molly was incredibly steadfast.

I slid into the drawing room with my painting and with great enthusiasm said, Benji, look! I painted our children.

Benjamin's mouth fixed itself into an "O," as did Mr. Bradley's and Mr. Lewis'. Reginald gave a wide-eyed grin. I liked Reginald, whomever he was.

"Er." Benjamin's eyebrows furrowed as he swallowed with a rather large gulp. "I beg your pardon, Miss Appleton?"

It was difficult not to burst out laughing at the men's reaction to my finger-painting, although it was easy to turn that deep emotion into a weep, as I already had impending tears in my eyes from nearly laughing. I pretended to look appalled and fell onto the sofa between Benjamin and Mr. Bradley, dropping my head into my hands.

"Good day, Ben," I heard one man say.

"I promised my mother that I would return home for tea," a closer voice said.

Benjamin begged, "Tobias, please–"

I then lifted my head to see Reginald reach for a biscuit

and then leave with the other two, thus leaving me alone with Benjamin.

Wonderful.

And Molly was doing brilliantly with my father.

I proceeded with my tears. "I cannot believe that the man I love would say such a thing!"

Benjamin placed a hand on my upper back in an attempt to be as comforting as he could possibly be, despite believing me to be mad. "No, it is lovely. I did not intend to upset you, my darling. Come, show me our *children*." I thought that he might be sick at saying the final word. I grinned to myself at the little victory.

I wiped my eyes with my hands and lifted the finger-painting off of the floor. Pointing to the first two figures and ignoring the question in his eyes asking why I had chosen this particular method of painting, I explained with false modesty "This is us." I shifted to the ten children along the canvas and named them one by one. "This is Benji II, Small Anna, Alabaster (Benjamin coughed), Eustace, Helga, Agatha, Horace, Rupert, Howard, and Mildred.

"I had not realised that women could *choose* sex of their children," Benjamin said as more of a question than a statement.

Surely, he was correct, but I immensely enjoyed teasing him. "Oh, we can. It is all in a woman's diet."

"That does not explain the unfortunate six wives of King Henry VIII."

"Oh," I brushed off his comment. "It is a new discovery. And besides, King Henry VIII was a madman."

"That, he was." At that, we laughed in unison and it was the first time, I realised, that I had not heard Benjamin's laugh since he had shoved a toad in my face. His laugh sounded like warm fudge.

"Is saying that treasonous?" I wondered aloud.

"No. He has nobody alive to protect his image."

"Not even the current King George?" We both laughed again and as we made eye contact, I realised I had forgotten my motive. Drat. I pointed back at the canvas of our children. "How soon after our marriage do you reckon that I might become with child?"

At that point, all laughing ceased and Benjamin choked.

I turned the canvas around to reveal a list that I had drawn out on the back with pastels then I cleared my throat. Benjamin took a long sip of his port. "The dates that I have pondered on goes as follows: Our honeymoon." Why Benjamin had not immediately swallowed his port post-sip, I was not sure, for his white cravat turned a shade of burgundy and he attempted to wipe at the incident with a handkerchief. I held back a chuckle. "February second."

"That is an awfully specific date," he commented.

I continued. "February third, February fifth, or February sixth."

"Why not February fourth?" He tried to sound interesting but I knew that he was not. He was horrified was what he was.

I shrugged. "Because I despise the number four."

"Is there a reason for that?"

Not particularly," I said nonchalantly.

I reckoned he had nothing more to say because he did not ask me any more questions.

CHAPTER 3

Day Three
7 Days Before Christmas Day

W hen I was a child, I had a doll that I had taken with me everywhere I went. The doll's name was Orange. One of the button eyes had torn off and the other eye was simply very loose, so I drew a smile on her face that had made her look entirely disproportionate. It had never had hair, so that gave me the perfect opportunity to ask Benjamin the most unsettling question he had ever heard in his life.

"I beg your pardon?"

"A lock of your hair," I said again. "For this doll. To give to our Benji II. So that even if you die, he always has his father with him."

A dismal comment to have made as Christmastide was approaching. Benjamin seemed to think so, scratching his head the way he did at the word, *die.*

He stared at the doll with a severely haunted look in his eye. "I do not see why we cannot simply give him a *new* doll.

Seeing as the child is not exactly born yet, I suppose that time is not of the essence.

I gasped much more theatrically than I ever had before. "But what if I wish to pass it down as an heirloom?"

Benjamin stepped forward to place his hands on my shoulders and look me in the eyes. In any normal circumstances with any other gentleman, I would have thought about this moment later and fallen into my bed, swooning like a rather infatuated blockhead. But alas, this was Benjamin and I did not care for the ridiculous man in a silly hat.

For those with significantly creative imaginations, it was a top hat that Benjamin wore. Although it might as well have been a jester's hat, for he must have fancied himself amusing enough to have the gall to choose me as a wife. Did he believe me to be susceptible to his no-good schemes? I knew Benjamin and I knew that if I married him, he would fill my life with punishment. For what, that was to be observed, as I had never done anything in my life to warrant such cruelty. But as a boy who'd been willing to tease me about a toad was a man willing to torment me.

At the idea, I wondered what I had done to upset my father enough for him to accept this proposal on my behalf. As his daughter, I knew that I was not completely innocent. *Completely.* I recalled a time when I was fifteen and I went to Town with Molly to avoid studying my Latin. But to marry me off to Benjamin Blackburn because of that? Surely my father had more sense than that.

To my comment concerning the word, *heirloom*, Benjamin said, "Might we have it *fixed* then?"

I held my hand to my heart. "*What* did you say!"

Benjamin cowered back with fear in his eyes. I might have laughed at him in any other circumstance that was not an important mission such as this. "That is to say, what a lovely idea!"

I chortled. Luckily, I was able to convince him that it was not out of mere frivolity, but holiday joy that he had just agreed. However, I was keenly aware that he was not truly in agreement, but obligation, what with being my intended and whatnot. Decidedly not for much longer. "I am glad that we understand each other, Benji!"

His smile said one thing, but his eyes said another. Of which was, "We do not understand one another."

Then, for the next item. Without warning, I lifted a potted plant from the table and thrusted it at him.

"A holly."

"As a symbol of our love," I explained. "It bloomed just before Christmastide."

"The holly or our love?" He asked.

"Both."

Benjamin bit his tongue, set the holly back in front of us, and said, "Ah."

I sighed, pleased.

CHAPTER 4

Day Four
6 Days Before Christmas Day

"Papa! Must I go?" Crying seemed a reasonable thing to do at this moment, but I reckoned that tears might have been a waste, as nobody had died.

My father, the confused man, stuttered a bit. "Of course!" He cleared his throat and sipped his tea. As did I. Tea, on these winter days, was refreshing not only because of the weather, but for other, rather absurd reasons. "This is, it is your choice, but as his intended, you are expected to make an appearance."

"But I have never been ice skating in all my life, Papa." I could have sworn that just like when Benjamin and I were children, and he had tried to force me to kiss a toad, that he was also trying to get me killed on the ice. He had enough gall to do that. Just before Christmastide, no less.

Horrid man!

"One is never too old to learn." As he said it, my father smirked and patted my head.

I blinked twice. "Papa! I am," I considered a moment,

having forgotten the year in which I was born. "I am seventeen. Had I wished to learn how to skate, I'd have done that years ago. I will fail now."

At that, my father retired from the drawing room, leaving not only me, but also his tea.

I frowned. Not because I was now sitting in the drawing room alone with an unlit hearth (my father favoured the cold) and tea; I frowned because I now felt obligated to learn how to ice skate with Benjamin. My fiance whom I did not wish to have a connection with. Odious man.

I needed Molly.

When I reached my bed-chamber, I flashed my lantern through my window pulling Molly's attention, too easily, as usual, from whatever it was that she was doing. I then scribbled my note.

Dearest Molly,

A tragedy has befallen me. I am to go ice skating with Mr. Blackburn at noon. A plan is gravely needed, lest I should die a most painful death.

Our trusted rock did not break a vase when thrown through Molly's open window. This time, she'd had the good sense to move anything of value or that, well, may break. Like a vase perchance. I did get no response back, for Molly decided to come over immediately and devise a plan. However, Molly *did* toss the rock back to my side of the cobblestone without warning. So, as to not receive a head injury, I ducked and the rock hit my closed door. I turned to scold Molly, but just as I did, her eyes widened with guilt, her face reddened, and she rushed out of her bedchamber.

I was uncertain if she was going to come over anymore, but I would find out in about two minutes unless my mother turned her away. Because, that is, I also heard the stomping of my father's feet approaching my bed-chamber.

For once, I considered that it might not be so bad to be married to Benjamin, for when a woman's father accuses her of being impetuous, it does not often make her wish to stay with him; it gives her a deep desire to prove that he is incorrect. It was Molly who threw the rock across the cobblestone, into my window, and at my door, not I. I did explain this to him, but he told me that we were fickle to even be throwing rocks into one another's bed-chambers in the first place. He also pointed out that the married woman that Molly was, she should have been wiser than to follow my example in throwing rocks.

I wanted to ask him why being married should have meant that she should not have thrown rocks, but before I could, he left me alone. Molly arrived with sugar plums an hour later as an apology for breaking my door with a rock, but she was quick to leave. No plan was devised, Unfortunately, it would be a simple day of the classical methods: pretending to be utterly uncouth at a skill. This would be easy seeing as I did not need to pretend; I was clumsy and I did not know how to ice skate.

Bones would likely be fractured.

Much like Molly's flower pot.

If I ought to have, I would have attended the Christmas ball with a splint on each limb so as to not marry Benjamin. The risks that I was willing to take were becoming dangerous by any means.

Perhaps that would have been a little too harsh. But in my defence, the pig had tried to force me to kiss a toad, among other things too grotesque to be noted. Toads had never been meant to be kissed by ladies of good breeding. I was of excellent breeding, so Benjamin really had never known me.

And so, I arrived at the lake to find Benjamin, his parents, his brother, and three strangers whom I had never seen before. My breath caught in my throat. Had I missed that his family would be there or had I simply ignored it? I was not entirely certain how I would be able to act like a fool with all of these people around.

Drat.

"This must be Miss Appleton!' One of the strangers–the old man–said. "What a pleasure to meet you today, my dear."

It was not my proudest moment, but my immediate response was, "Rubbish." The remaining people, including Benjamin, stared over at me with question in their eyes. I thought up a response to quickly fix myself. "That is, it is a pleasure to meet *you*, Mr.—"

"Anna, this is my uncle, Abraham," Benjamin cut in. I found myself grateful for the interruption, then I scolded myself for having a kind thought about him. *Naughty, Anna!* "And you know my brother, Alexander. This is his wife, Grace, and their daughter Georgiana. Benjamin's niece grasped his leg with affection. The sweet gesture warmed my heart. I did tend to have a fondness for children; I only wished that it was not a Blackburn child.

"Have you been skating before, Miss Anna?" asked Mr. Blackburn (the father).

I hesitated. "Why, yes I have." The important thing was that I smiled, so nobody could see my hesitation.

Except. Perhaps. Benjamin. The suspicion in his eyes was vexing.

"Oh, lovely!" Mrs. Blackburn clapped her hands and went forth onto the frozen lake with Mr. Blackburn and the rest of Benjamin's family, leaving me alone with him.

"I suppose I will help you into your skates then," he said.

Had I known how to fasten my own skates, I'd have refused his offer to help, but I, to my grave disappointment had not the slightest idea how to fasten my skates, for, as previously mentioned, I had never before been ice skating and I preferred to have well-tied skates over ill-tied ones that might have made me slip and fall on my nose. And so, I stretched my leg toward Benjamin as he bent in front of me and allowed him access to my first foot. "You have never gone ice skating in all your life," Benjamin commented nonchalantly as he picked up one of my skates—or rather my mother's skate.

"Rubbish!" Benjamin snorted in response. "I have skat-edgot skating plenty of times."

"Then fasten your own skates."

"Indeed, I will *not* fasten my own skate, you underbred..." I searched for a word. "*Ninny!*"

Benjamin's eyes widened as he cocked his head back, clearly caught off guard. After a moment, Benjamin came forward and patted my foot. "It was only a suggestion." The look that he gave me as he tightened my shoelaces irked me. I kicked off his hand and while he blinked, he backed off and said nothing; he only watched me as I *hmphed* and fastened my own skate, as well as the next skate with a foolish smirk upon his pesky face. "Your skates are too loose," he said. "You're going to fall."

"Oh, rubbish!" I raised my hands for him to take. "Now, please help me towards the ice, my love."

My too-attentive fiancé attended to me all too well and it was vexing. His hold on me as he led me to the ice was strong, willing to fall with me if it came to itI fell, but unwilling to let go. His grip was also warm and comforting. While it was indeed vexing, my stomach seemed to favour it.

Until his niece swiped by and snatched him from me, henceforth leaving me frozen. I believe that I heard him snicker menacingly. I also shook and not because of the weather; the weather was relatively non bothersome at this point in time; I was afraid. I watched my legs as I willed them to stay put because I would not be skating past this point.

No, that I would not do. No, no, no.

I needed a distraction.

I glanced up from my feet to my deplorable fiancé as he— *oh*—spun around on the ice dancing with Georgiana. Somehow, I could not despise a man for sharing a tender moment like this even though he had left me in the middle of a frozen lake.

And then, with the luck of an insect, I became a stinging, wet mess; due credit to that toad!

"B-Benj-jamin B-Blackb-burn, y-you d-desp-picab-ble man." He could have been holding me as close to his abnormally warm chest as wanted to, but I would never forgive him, even if I did ever become warm again.

He worsened his case because he laughed. He laughed! "I am truly sorry, Anna."

"I-It is M-Miss A-Applet-ton t-to y-you!"

"Benny, how could you have allowed this to happen?" His mother scolded him severely as his family followed behind us on the way to their home. I might have laughed if I'd had it in me.

"Honestly, Son. She is your fiancée for goodness' sake," his father added.

His uncle remained silent. As did Alexander and his wife. Georgiana seemed to care very little.

Benjamin's face reddened much more than it already was from the cold winter air. I almost felt bad for him. I might have if I had not just fallen through the ice! "It will never happen again, Miss Appleton. I should've been paying more attention to you."

I was so angry with Benjamin that I said nothing in response.

"Good heavens. Are you all right, Miss Appleton?" Mrs. Blackburn asked.

I felt that I needed to respond to Benjamin's mother, for she had done nothing and she did not deserve my rudeness. "Oh, I have never been better, Mrs. Blackburn." I might've come up with something better; obviously, it was a lie seeing as I had just fallen through ice and I was shivering.

"Rubbish," Benjamin said, eyeing me.

That man! "*R-Rub-bbish,*" I retorted. He would not steal my word!

"Rubbish."

"Rub-bbish!"

"Rubb*ish.*"

"R-RUBBISH."

"*Les déchets.*" Now, he was making this unfair! I was only advanced in French, so I had no other language to fall on.

The shivering would need to cease for a moment.

"RUBBISH, RUBBISH, RUBBISH, RUBBISH, RUBBISH, RUBBISH!"

"RUBBISH, RUBBISH, RUBBISH, RUBBISH, RUBBISH, RUBBISH!"

CHAPTER 5

Day Five

5 Days Before Christmas Day

"Whatever do you mean that you are averse to eating meat?" Mrs. Blackburn was aghast.

"I am only considering the animals, Ma'am," I said, pretending to be emotional as I stared at the vegetables that the goose would soon be placed by. "The poor thing must have been minding his own business only to have some beast sneak up on him and lop his head off!" For effect, I punched the table, starling Benjamin's niece; she returned to eating her bread. Meanwhile, Benjamin's head fell into his hand, but I could not tell if he was laughing or not. "And to have his feathery friends watch!"

"Miss Appleton. Alex killed the goose," said Mrs. Blackburn.

Things became awkward at that moment and I was therefore at a loss for words. "Er…"

"We will accommodate you, Miss Appleton." Mrs. Blackburn was not as excellent as I in the art of playing make-believe, so she was quite obviously perplexed and incredibly nettled, but she would not have had me know that. Poor, blessed woman.

I threw my hands up in some haphazard manner. "Oh, no, no. I will fill myself up with bread. I do not wish to be any trouble to you." A lie, for I did. I felt Benjamin's meticulous stare on me, so in return, I glared at him harshly to distract myself from the feeling down my arms and neck. "I think that bread is a perfectly decent meal."

Mrs. Blackburn disregarded me sort of like my father had when I told him that I did not wish to marry Benjamin Blackburn: she lifted her finger at me. "Oh, nonsense. Cook!" The women disappeared from the table into–I presume–the kitchen, in seconds.

Benjamin leaned nearer to me and his voice ticked my ear. "I believe that I recall you eating pheasant once."

He was anticipating my scheme!

"You are mistaken. Meat-eating makes me ill," I argued. Catch me in the lie, he would not. "Besides, you have not been in my company for at least a decade."

"I still have a clear memory of the time, Anna."

Remembering that it was *pheasant meat* suggested that it was true, as it likely was pheasant meat, for my Great Uncle Richard often hunted pheasants until he tragically died two years prior when one landed on his head after he shot it while hunting one afternoon. He was a frail man, so the bird's weight had not been merciful.

As I pondered on that dear man and his pursuits, Mrs. Blackburn returned to the dining table and sat at the opposite end of her husband as she had been before. Oftentimes, when a person entered a room, they greeted their surrounding counterparts, however, Mrs. Blackburn's lips remained free of words and only opened when she sipped her cider. Cook traipsed in a moment later with the aforementioned goose, finely cooked, and–was it as spoiled as it smelled? The goose that I had eaten before had never smelled so foul that way that I recalled it. Perhaps it was fortuitous that Mrs. Blackburn had requested an alternative meal for me.

Cook set the rancid bird at the centre of the table beside the bread, the vegetables, and the jellies then disappeared back into the kitchen, returning with a bowl soon thereafter. Placed in front of me was the bowl filled with a milky -yellow-green soup.

If it was not my own worst enemy (except Benjamin) staring me in the face.

Pease soup.

I would eat this until the bowl was stripped of colour, but that did not mean that I would enjoy it. Heavens, this act was beginning to seem absurd.

When Cook curtsied to us and went off, I heard a slight snort beside me. I leaned over and muttered, "At least I will not be eating a putrid bird that was executed in front of his family."

"Well, that *putrid bird* was a female called Peggy, and she happens to have been fed very well for the very purpose of being eaten today, so she is sure to be quite flavourful." His smile was so wicked that I wanted to flick his nose. He knew what I was playing at; he knew that I would have rather eaten the goose than the soup. Benjamin Blackburn was teasing me!

In a perfect world. I would not have scalded my tongue on Pease soup and I would not be in the exact position. Yet, I was, and Benjamin happened to know about that particular incident because it was during Mr. and Mrs. Cooper's village Christmastide dinner a year prior and he had happened to be sitting near me when I had wailed.

I cleared my throat, truthfully bothered, and then picked up my spoon. I happen to be looking forward to eating this soup." Just when I dipped my spoon into the green cruelty of my soup, Benjamin interrupted me.

"Grace first, Anna."

Grace?

Ah, *Grace.*

"Oh, yes." I hastily sat down my spoon and everybody around the table held hands. As Elder Mr. Blackburn prayed, I frowned, thankful that nobody was able to see me. My family had seldom shared a meal in seven years and when we did, we did not hold hands around the table to pray; we did not even say Grace. If our meal was to be blessed, it was blessed individually. Of course, there was still love in my home, but the love in Benjamin's home was different somehow and I rather enjoyed how different it was.

Upon saying "Amen," I lifted my spoon and tried, once more, to eat my soup. It was warm, but not nearly as boiling as the soup that Mr. and Mrs. Cooper had served. I was willing to wager that it was better than the goose as well. I stared at the goose as I ate my soup.

Seemingly, Benjamin noticed my stare at it, so he teased me. "Would you like some? Or will it make you weep?"

"I am fine, Benji."

"Alex," Benjamin spoke suddenly past the discussion between their parents and Georgiana. My attention switched from my Pease soup to Benjamin and Alexander faced him seconds later. "Do you remember the last time that we ate goose?"

Afraid, Alexander looked between me and his brother then he begged, "Benjamin, no."

Benjamin dismissed Alexander and grinned wickedly at me. I found myself rather excited to hear about the last time Alexander ate goose. "He vomited, Anna." The discussion between Mr. and Mrs. Blackburn ceased and they, in addition to Alexander's wife and daughter, faced Benjamin in consternation. I, however, lost my ability to eat my *green* soup so I pushed it away, and poor, embarrassed Alexander dropped his head into his hands with a heavy sigh.

"Ben!" Exhausted his mother. In all fairness, he was embarrassing his brother.

"My heavens." I cleared my throat. "Please, dear, tell me more."

"Well," Benjamin clapped his hands together, watching me carefully. Why, I did not know, but it made me rather nervous. "It was his first time eating it and he's already been a little ill earlier that day, so the blasted smell made him vomit—"

"Ben," Mr. Blackburn tried to interject.

"—all over the dinner table."

I wondered if I was green because now, it was I that the Blackburn family was laughing at. I tried to turn the attention away from me. "I am sorry that Benji told me that, Mr. Blackburn. Had I known how much it might humiliate you, I'd have not allowed him to tell me."

"You're to be my sister-in-law." This, I found I did not hate the sound of. "He's destined to tell you all sorts of things about me. Don't apologise," Alexander smiled at me kindly and I believed it to have ended the discussion, but then Benjamin leaned over to me and I lost feeling in my toes.

"What a delightful game."

Drat.

Benjamin knew what I was doing.

I took tea with the two Mrs. Blackburns in the parlour after dinner while the men took their liquor elsewhere and Georgiana was led to the nursery by a maid. "Despite the unimpressive display earlier," said the elder Mrs. Blackburn. "Benjamin is quite fond of you, Miss Appleton."

I set down my tea. "What has brought you to this conclusion, Ma'am?" He was positively only trying to torture me.

"He watches you. Have you not noticed?" This was probably the first thing that I'd heard Grace say.

"Certainly not."

"Well, he does. He has ever since the two of you were children," said Mrs. Blackburn.

Grace added, "He wants to make such a nice life for you."

"Have the two of you discussed your wedding date?" One of them asked. I couldn't decipher which one because I was intrigued about how they seemed to be so certain of Benjamin's intentions and feelings.

"Hardly," I said honestly. We'd talked very little about our present circumstances. "I only know when we'll announce it, so I think the middle of January might be lovely. And just long enough for the banns to have been put up."

"Oh, I cannot tell you how much I am anticipating that day!" This came from Mrs. Blackburn.

I was angry because, at some point during tea, I found myself feeling the same way.

CHAPTER 6

Day Six
4 Days Before Christmas Day

I knew that outside the door were wassailers due to the lively singing of, "While Shepherds Watched Their Flocks by Night" that I could hear from the drawing room. They were rather loud and I did not wish to stand by the door and listen to them sing, giving the winter breeze allowance into the house.

It was cold enough inside, credit to my father.

My mother and father, however, loved when the wassailers came. and they were thrilled to have a listen.

Perhaps setting down my cider and slipping out the back door without my coat or bonnet had been foolish and antichrist, but the wassailers came every year, several times. I was not going to miss anything of great importance. My first thought once I was safely outside was to make haste to Benjamin's house. I might have gone to see Molly as a first resort, but I could not have known if the wassailers had passed by her house yet. I was not going to escape, only to still put myself into danger. Considering that we all lived in the village, Benjamin's house was not far from my own; most days, I wished that I lived somewhere more captivating, like London, but today I was glad to live where I did.

In approximately two minutes, I arrived at Benjamin's and I knocked on the door. Mr. Alexander Blackburn, rather than the butler they were fortuitous enough to afford, opened the door and he immediately fell into confusion. I could not blame him, however, I said, "I am his fiance. Unannounced visits will happen on occasion." I shivered and remembered that I had no coat.

Perhaps *that* was the cause of Alexander's confusion.

Alexander blinked. He blinked again. "I see. Well, Ben had taken leave to The Sequoia."

I shivered once more. "He is not here?" I might as well have cried the last word out, as it came with great pain in my voice.

"I am sure that he won't mind you joining him," Alexander suggested. "But first, wait here." He left me standing outside their home in the cold for reasons unknown. I hoped that it would not be for long. I reared my head back a little to find the wassailers. They were *still* singing to my parents! Alexander returned and I quickly fixed my head. He handed over a neatly folded holly red garment. "This is my wife's. Ben will kill me if I send you without a coat."

Or, rather, for sending me *with* a coat.

I wrapped the coat around myself and I felt a relief at the warmth it brought me. Alexander still watched me like I was a bat in the daytime. "Wassailers," I explained.

Alexander chuckled. "You need not explain anything to *me,* Miss Appleton." he shut the door in my face, leaving me to find Benjamin at The Sequoia. Why was he at The Sequoia? Was it some refuge of his that I would be invading? I suddenly felt that I should not find him, but then reminded myself why I should: Reason one, to escape the horrors of wassailers. Reason two fell at the prospect of angering him, thus having the engagement ended. I placed my hands in the pockets of the coat only to find black gloves. At this, I laughed.

It was not amusing, but it was convenient. I pulled the gloves onto my hands and made my way to find Benjamin. To my great luck, the way to The Sequoia did not require me to pass by my house again; there was no way of knowing if my parents were still listening to the wassailers. I did hear them in the distance, though, above the light winds. They were singing "The First Noel"." It was a song hardly familiar to me. I had heard it five years before when my parents and I had taken a trip to Cornwall during Christmastide, but that had been the only time I had heard it until now.

I found Benjamin just where Alexander had told me to look. At The Sequoia. He was leaning against it and smoking a cigar. I scrunched my nose, for I hated that smell. My Great Uncle Richard had taken the habit of smoking before his untimely demise and I often left the room when I did because the smell had been disagreeable to me. I made my way towards Benjamin, but he did not need to glance up to know it. "Afternoon, Anna."

He sounded rather... *Not angry.*

"I am surprised that you have sought me out," he added with amusement in his voice. He lifted his head from the tree then he blew out a ring of smoke in my general direction. The whisper of the horrid scent was not pleasing.

"T'is a filthy habit, Benji," was what I said in response.

He was unaffected. "Is it?" He took another puff to spite me, but he turned his head to blow it in a separate direction from my face. I appreciated that greatly.

"Yes." I did not know what else to say. In response, Benjamin dropped the cigar into the snow and stomped on it.

Apparently not much needed to be said. "You are not going to argue?"

"If my fiancee wishes me to stop then I will not continue." Benjamin shrugged. "Do you need something?"

"I am merely escaping the Hounds of musical Hell."

"I beg your pardon?"

"The wassailers."

Benjamin nodded once. "Ah. I can say the same."

"They have already passed by your house?"

"A few hours ago." What a long time to be out in weather like this. "I slipped out a window."

Relief unwillingly filled my soul. "You are not angry that I am here then?"

"Why should I be?" he asked with genuine curiosity.

"Perhaps you wished to be left alone and I ruined it."

Benjamin huffed a laugh. "Hardly. Besides, I have already spent my time alone." He then scanned me from head to foot and I stood in confusion, waiting for him to say more. "Why are you wearing Grace's coat and gloves?"

A reasonable question.

"Er..."

"You failed to dress appropriately for the weather in your rush to leave the wassailers, I bet," Benjamin smirked at me. The fool was correct. "You showed up at my house and she let you borrow them."

"It was your brother," I corrected. Otherwise, nothing else could be correct; Benjamin could read my like the *Castle Combe Chronicle*. It was unsettling

Benjamin lifted his entire body from The Sequoia and I unreadily caught my breath imagining how his biceps bulged through his coat. I knew they had because they often did similar movements. "We should get you home then. Grace will want those back. Chances are, Alex did not ask for permission and while I must protect *you*, I must also protect my brother from his wife's wrath."

Grace had wrath?

That question sitting in my mind, I found that I did not want to go home. "What if the wassailers are still there?"

Benjamin pulled his pocket watch from his coat pocket. "What time did they show up?"

"A quarter after three."

Benjamin glanced at me through his eyelashes. "Anna, it is a quarter to four now. I doubt they are still there." I supposed the excuse was not so brilliant. "Come." Benjamin offered me his arm and I took it. He guided me through the snow until we were on the cobblestone. We strolled at a leisurely pace.

"Why me?" I had not meant to say it out loud.

I felt Benjamin tense. "What do you mean?"

I tried my best to cover up my question. I could not bear being told that I was merely convenient or some other such thing. "That is, why did you choose the winter to get married?"

Benjamin cleared his throat. "Because you look beautiful in the winter." I felt as though I were melting. That was the kindest thing he had ever said to me. "I cannot explain it lest I wish to sound like a nut."

"No, please explain it. I will not laugh," I begged. I needed to know.

He was not quite so difficult to convince. "Fine." Benjamin led us to a bench and we sat beside each other. He looked me in the eyes as he spoke. You seem *lighter* somehow, in the winter. Especially the way your cheeks and nose redden when you're outside."

I blew off his last comment. "Everybody's face reddens in the winter, Benji."

"Not like yours."

Oh, good heavens. He had answered every question that I'd been wondering about.

Benjamin Blackburn chose *me* because he fancied me. He never wanted to torture me and if he ever was to, it was because he fancied me. Did he know that I was trying to push him away? He knew that I was playing a game, but perhaps not the idea of the game. I'd always played games as a child and apparently, he had watched me enough to know that. Not to mention the time we spent together until we were eight.

Did I quit my scheme and just marry the poor man, or continue?

I needed to consult Molly.

CHAPTER 7

Day Seven
3 Days Before Christmas Day

According to Molly, I was to continue my scheme. I would finish what I started. Just because he cared about me, it did not mean that *I* should be unhappily married in the way that Molly was. My future was mine and I would not give it away unless I loved Benjamin too. Although it was becoming more of a possibility the more I spent time with him, it would not happen. Teasing a girl by way of a toad was no way to earn her affection.

At the thought of toads and, in turn, warts, I considered Benjamin's mole. As a child, Benjamin had a large mole on his chin; he had looked rather haggard. However, either said mole had become smaller, his head had grown, or I had simply been ignorant of it for the last six days, for it had not been quite as much of a distraction of late. Unfortunately, Benjamin looked less haggard and significantly more handsome.

Beside me, facing the hearth where the fire burned, telling

us that Christmastide was near, I was drinking tea with Molly and Benjamin. I had not expected Molly to visit, but when she had told me that her husband was going to be in London for two days on business, I had invited her to stay, much contradicting my father's requests that I should not be distracted by my friend during this "most fortuitous time." He very well knew not how involved dear Molly truly was and about that, I was delighted.

"Benji, my dear," I said prior to taking a sip of tea.

"Yes?" He watched me take my sip and swallow it.

"I see that you have grown into your mole." Molly turned her head away and I watched her head bob a little. Meanwhile, Benjamin's mouth hung open. I entertained a bee flying inside, but seeing that it was not summertime, I pushed the thought aside. I did not imagine Benjamin knew how to respond, so I continued. "I suppose that it will forever be taking its refuge on your face and *mole* is such a grotesque word, so paying mind to that..." Benjamin watched me as though I was a miraculous partridge in the sky. "I propose that we name it."

"Name it, you say?" I could not tell if he liked the idea or if he detested it. I affirm that there must have been a hint of a grin on his face.

I nodded once. "Name it, I say," I confirmed.

"And what, Anna, am I to name my mole?" He sat tall as though he were a proud child waiting for a reward.

What escaped my mouth next was not under my control. "Madam Francesca."

Benjamin snorted and then he erupted with a laughter so infectious that Molly joined him and I scooted back so as to not catch the infection. I was better than that; well, not better than Molly, bless her heart, but better than becoming ill.

"*Madam Francesca?*" Benjamin queried. Pursing my lips, I nodded. "Why, may I ask?"

"The truth of it all was that of Francesca Bellingham. Madam Bellingham had been my French tutor when I'd been all but eight and she'd been dismissed by my father after performing corporal punishment on me each time I pronounced a French word incorrectly. It was only my hands, although being clubbed with a wooden stick *anywhere* is not a comfortable feeling and it often leaves one's limbs red. When Madam Bellingham was approached by my father about the state of my hands, she'd told him in her curled "R's" and missing "H's" that there was no better way to learn a language than by firm discipline.

Les déchets.

My father personally showed her out and did not allow her to take her bags. The following week, Madam Petit who was every bit fitted for the name charmed the nursery with her gentle demeanour. I learned French quickly with her as my tutor.

I searched for a reason for naming Benjamin's mole Madam Francesca. That was *not* because she was a very despised person in the same way that I remembered Benjamin despising his mole. No other reason came.

"Anna," Benjamin proceeded. I tilted my head to the left waiting for him to say more. I also scratched my arm. "Are you so disturbed by my mole that you feel the motive to name it after your horrendous French tutor of 1807?"

Oh, merciful heavens, he knew!

"The first tutor," I corrected him in something much like a whisper. Then I realised the next part of his statement and gasped. "I am *not* disturbed by your mole!" Molly poured more tea into her cup.

"Is that so?" I did not nod because I was focused on the fact that his voice broke on the last word. He was amused. Drat. "If you are suggesting that *I* am bothered by it, I assure you that I am not. I rarely think about it."

"That is a good thing. Now, I should think that this discussion is concluded. Good day, Benji." I said it all in one breath then stood up to leave the room. "Come, Molly," I ordered, passing by her.

"Anna?"

"MOLLY, COME!"

I felt Benjamin's stare on my back before I disappeared behind the wall.

Me, as well as Molly, were frightened by my father's voice as we made our way up the stairs. "What do you think you are doing, Anna?"

I swallowed. "Er."

"You are not leaving Mr. Blackburn alone in the drawing room, are you?"

I faked a laugh. "No." A snort came from the drawing room. That odious man!

My father folded his arms. "Then where are you going?"

Molly and I shared a look as though she could give me an idea without words being spoken. "I..." I cleared my throat. "I must deal with some... Personal business."

At that, my father sighed and muttered, "Married life will do her well." Then he said, "And the can is in your bed-chamber?"

"Of course not, Father." I headed the correct way, with my father watching, Molly staying behind. With his keen ability to compel me in one way or the other, I was forced to remain in the drawing room with Benjamin after I returned from the john.

I was fortunate that Benjamin mentioned nothing of Madam Francesca.

Upon Benjamin taking his leave, I went to bed only to find Molly sleeping in my room. It seemed that I would be sleeping in the guest chamber for the night.

Instead of sleeping, I pondered on more schemes. Christmas Day and thus, the ball was in three days.

I was running out of time.

CHAPTER 8

Day Eight
2 Days Before Christmas Day

It was to be Christmas Eve the following day; Christmastide would soon arrive *and I was still engaged.* Most unfortunate.

Molly was at the ballet with her husband, so she was unable to assist me in my scheme today. It was all on me, and when I needed to think, there was no better place to do so than sitting near the pianoforte. In the Town the week previous to this one, I found new sheet music filled with many carols, my favourite one included: *Hark, the Herald Angels Sing.* There was simply no possible reason that I should have left it at the shop.

Following tea, I made my way to the music room to play on the pianoforte. When I pressed down on the first note, I paused. It came to mind that I had not played in quite some time, for I was usually with Molly while her husband was none but a boring man. It was a lovely sound, the pianoforte. I continued, stumbling a bit, but playing rather well, as I had gotten much practice as a girl seeing as my mother hardly let my siblings and I step away from our chosen instrument.

Except Mathilda. Charles and I wagered that she was the favourite child, for she was free as a mouse. The seven others thought that Charles and I were absurd, but that was why I usually forgot about the seven others and Charles shipped himself off to Europe for a year. I looked forward to penning him about my current misadventure with Benjamin Blackburn. I imagined that he would laugh. The thought made me smile as I played my music.

I needed to come up with a plan now.

"You play lovely, Anna."

That was when my fingers stumbled over the keys so dearly that it was impossible to brush over them. It seemed that I was overruled.

I turned to face him directly. "What in Heaven's name are you doing here?" I asked Benjamin with utmost sincerity. He had not even sent word of his unwelcome visit. "I am trying to practise," I lied. Trying to think, more like.

"I would love to sit and listen," he said wickedly. He knew that I did not want him here. Meanwhile, my heart dropped to my chest. He wished to hear me play; what glorious faith in me he had.

Oh.

He had faith in my piano skills.

From within, I laughed. "By all means, dear." I then turned towards the instrument once more and began. It was quite a deficient performance of *Adestes Fideles* and I imagined Benjamin's face twisting in all sorts of unexplainable, irreversible directions.

It didn't.

Upon turning back to look at him, I noticed a rather *peaceful* countenance in Benjamin. His cheeks were even pink as though he were still outside.

Drat. That nuisance.

"That was spectacular," Benjamin said. "Will you play more?"

I could not combat what I blurted out next. "BENJI! IT WAS DREADFUL!"

The gleam in Benjamin's eyes told me that he knew exactly what I was doing. Curse that goose dinner for challenging my act.

"Hardly," he brushed it off. "Please play more, dear."

I played *Joy to the World* off-key and at the wrong end of the piano. It should have injured his hearing as it had mine, although it did not. That is, he pretended that it did not. He was such a rude man.

When I finished though, Benjamin did not cheer or praise me; he huffed a laugh. "We do not need to get married if you wish *this badly* to get out of it."

At this, I choked on my tongue. *Proceed with the act. Make him go mad.* I practically fell from the piano bench and crawled to Benjamin's chair on all fours. "WHAT DO YOU MEAN THAT I DO NOT WISH TO MARRY YOU?" I asked him, pleadingly.

"Firstly, I have heard you play on the pianoforte and it is not nearly this awful," he winked at me. "Secondly, I know you enjoy meat and that you have no qualms about hunting. You also do not like being told what to do." About that, he was quite correct! "But if the toad incident is enough for you to punish me, then so be it. Know that your father was the arranger of this marriage though. I simply agreed to it because I like you enough."

Everything that I had assumed about him changed. It was all my father's doing! He had been pushing to marry me off enough that I should have known, yet I'd assumed it had been Benjamin's idea all because of *the toad incident*. I cleared my throat and without looking at him, said, "That is a curious reason to agree to matrimony."

"Well, you're an interesting woman, so it's fitting." I could hear him fighting a laugh. "I will release you from it if you get off of the floor."

I was not certain what I wanted anymore, but seeing as the floor was no ideal place to have a discussion, I did get up and sat back down on the piano bench. Perhaps I should have been glad to be relieved of the obligation, but alas, I felt that I needed to try harder; he had backed down too easily and not for his own sanity.

And so, I begged. "BUT BENJI! YOU ARE THE LOVE OF MY LIFE." Then I gasped. "Oh, dearest, do not let the children hear you!"

Benjamin blinked and then scanned the room. "Where are they?" Good heavens, why did he not seem perplexed?

"Well, they are watching over us. Awaiting their conception, you see."

"Watching over us?" Benjamin seemed greatly amused now.

I nodded.

"Have a lovely evening, Anna." He leaned over and kissed my cheek, then he retired from the music room and soon, the house.

CHAPTER 9

Day Nine
1 Day Before Christmas Day
Christmastide Begins

"**B**ENJAMIN BLACKBURN, YOU DESPICABLE MAN!" To my left, I heard my father emerging from his study.

"What the devil—" Then he saw it. The puppy in my arms had been delivered by Benjamin himself before he'd left me standing alone in the foyer with a Pomeranian in my arms and not a single idea of what I should do next. A snort emerged from the depths of my father's throat and I wondered how I managed to have *two* men in my laugh who snorted when they laughed. "He must care for you a great deal." He stepped closer to pet the Pomeranian's head. "Have you named it?"

"Er..." I looked from the puppy to my father, back to the puppy, and back to my father. "I have hardly had a moment." In fact, I considered the possibility that it was not really a gift for me like what Benjamin said; he was apt to fool me.

"Should I not return it?" How had Benjamin known of my adoration for Pomeranians?

"Don't return a gift, you silly girl!" Oh dear. He had gotten himself attached to the puppy *already.*

"But I have never named anything in all my life." I did not quite know how to remedy this situation.

"To start, what did Blackburn say of the sex?"

I shrugged. "He handed it to me and left laughing."

"How curious," my father smirked. "Lift it." I did. "Ah, a male."

"I see." That did nothing to help in naming the creature. However, I had one more chance to push Benjamin away. *Benedict.*

But he'd given me a puppy! The very kind of puppy that I'd been forced to return to her owners when I was all but four. Quite clearly, it seemed, Benjamin had remembered that gloomy day.

I said the second name that came to mind. "Pip." In a moment of realisation whilst staring at the puppy, my eyes welled up. "Pip!"

My father set a hand on my shoulder. "I'd wager that Blackburn is expecting you by now."

"I rather think that he might be." At that, I made my way to scold Mr. Blackburn for being the most brilliantly kind base miscreant in my life. I knocked on the front door with great aim.

Within seconds, Benjamin was standing in front of me grinning like he was preparing to tell me some silly joke. "Hello again, Anna. Is the Pomeranian not to your liking?"

"How did you manage it?"

"Do you remember–"

"Yes, I do," I cut him off. "But that is not my question."

Benjamin chuckled to himself and stepped outside, crossing his arms in an attempt to block them somewhat from the bitter air. "Your father has connections, and so we were able to conspire and obtain this purebred Pomeranian."

My father knew? That must have been why he did not seem at all shocked when he'd come from his study to see me with an animal. I scanned Pip. "He looks nearly identical to her." I said, having just noticed it."How did you manage that?"

"He is the grandson of that one."

I nearly began to cry at the thought. "Is she–"

"No, she is well. She *is* old, however." Benjamin petted up and down Pip's back. "What have you named him?"

"Pip."

Benjamin hmphed. "Fitting."

I could not possibly leave him for the day without thanking him, so after staying on the front porch conversing for some time, I turned to leave. "Thank you, Benjamin."

"It is only the first day of Christmas." Benjamin winked.

"There are only twelve days," I corrected him.

"Yes, well, you deserve an extra day." I had no choice but to argue or simply leave. I was exhausted, so I chose the latter. "I will see you at the ball tomorrow. Big day, it is. I reckon."

"Yes, a big day," I said without thinking about what exactly would happen at the ball.I also had to think about a gift for him that was a match for Pip.

I had never been good with planning. But then, Benjamin's influence on the holidays this year was not meant to be so grand.

CHAPTER 10

Day Ten
Christmas Day

T he ball was held at the Cooper's. Their home was the largest in the village, so it only made sense for them to host the ball each year. I only arrived much later than my family and Molly because I spent the morning panicking.

This event was my last opportunity to make Benjamin cower and only had an hour or two to manage it. Yet, I had not seen Molly in several days and therefore, I knew not what scheme to pull. I was out of ideas and I was not quite as determined to bring the engagement to an end anymore. Only because I needed to do what I would do without destroying Benjamin's pride.

Or feelings, at that.

Even though I was late, I was ready to leave, as Mathilda had helped me do so. The dress I was wearing was a soft yellow and I had three holly berries in my curled hair. The berries had been entirely Mathilda's idea and, as she was styling my hair, I made certain to assure her that she'd be getting around with a splint on both of her legs for the next little while if the berries wound up crushed and thus dying my blonde locks crimson.

Mathilda, with her much darker hair and without the same worries as I, responded by informing me that in that event, my hair would not be dyed permanently. How she knew this, I pondered on for quite a while.

The entire village was crowding the Cooper's home when I arrived. It seemed that I was the only person who was late. I searched for Molly first and foremost, and when I was distracted by a particular and particularly dashing gentleman in the corner, I reminded myself of my motive. I waved over to Molly as I made my way to her. "MOLLY!"

Molly was quick to glance over at her name and find me. She smiled and met me halfway. "You look lovely, Anna."

"Yes, yes, as do you," was my quick response then I followed, distressed, with. "What shall I do?"

"You're still engaged?"

I groaned. "Molly, if I was not, you'd be the first to know."

"He must like you immensely," Molly said with utmost joy and satisfaction.

"Molly, it is not good! He got me a puppy for goodness' sake!"

Molly gasped, cupping her hand over her mouth. "Is it a Pomeranian?" I nodded. She performed a slight dance. "He is entirely smitten. Please put a stop to your scheme," she begged.

"But Molly–"

"Anna." Molly placed a hand on my shoulder. "You will never be bored with him. That is more than anybody can ask for."

Perhaps she had a point. I contemplated Molly's marriage to the bore, then on my father who was not entirely boring, but also had no time for games, then on Benjamin. Nary was there ever a dull moment with that toad. I glanced over to where I had seen Benjamin as I entered the ball to see that he was still there.

With Angela Birmingham.

And he was laughing at something she'd said.

Angela, that ox!

I then gasped when I noticed a mistletoe above them. The Coopers, those schemers! I'd never known them to wish to cause a scandal, yet here at their ball, was a dratted mistletoe. Nothing was as it seemed anymore.

Without thinking, I found myself stomping over to Benjamin with my hands clenched into fists. This would *not* happen. He would not be swiped away by Angela Birmingham in front of my very eyes.

When I reached Benjamin, I pulled on his cravat and pulled him down to me. What I did next caught the attention of each party guest.

I kissed Benjamin underneath the mistletoe.

The guests all gasped in harmony. I felt that I should have been stunned that, even in front of everybody, Benjamin did not pull me away. He pulled me closer in some sort of embrace. I was more than happy to be in this particular position.

This scandalous position.

Oh dear. Everything was ruined!

I pushed Benjamin back and took in all of our surroundings. My father and my mother were glaring at me, my siblings were not exactly paying attention, Molly's jaw had fallen so far that it seemed she may not be able to return it to its natural state, and Benjamin's family was jovial at the performance. The rest of the guests that were watching, however, pretended like they cared with their hands clasped over their mouths. Holding back tears, I looked between Benjamin and Angela, my gaze falling on Benjamin. "I am sorry."

Unable to handle the attention any longer, I turned away

from Benjamin and ran at the front door. I needed to go home and sit in front of the fire with Pip and refused to speak to my younger siblings.

Just before I dashed out of the house, I heard Benjamin shout, "Miss Appleton!" as he chased me away from the party. I itched to wipe the tears from my face, but that would only have slowed me down, so I tried to ignore them and I sped up.

I gave it up when my panting became heavy and I felt that I might faint. Benjamin found me underneath the Sequoia where I'd ordered him to put out his cigar only a few days before and he'd obeyed.

In front of me was a man who cared and it was just as inevitable as birth and death.

"Where are you going?" Benjamin asked me in heavy breaths. Though I wasn't looking at him, I felt his hard stare.

"I am going home." My voice was raspier than I'd have liked.

Benjamin sighed. "Anna. Why are you so determined to get out of this engagement?"

It should not have, but his question took me by surprise. "I am not."

For the first time during our arrangement, Benjamin was not amused by something I said or did. "Confess." I wanted to tell him what an odious toad he was, or had been as a child, but I found that I couldn't say it because it was not true anymore. Benjamin was affectionate and caring. "It is obvious that you have been trying to frighten me out of a marriage with you, but I think you have found that it is impossible."

"That is because you are trying to uphold my father's wishes to marry me off. I am not your problem, Ben!"

Benjamin's tone remained the same. "I am not simply trying to please your father by marrying you. If I had any other lady's father come to me and ask me to marry her, I'd have said no because *they* are not my problem. However, I made *you* my problem many years ago."

Had I been in a more romantic mood, I might have fainted from that confession. He'd only accepted it because of me. "Then why did you not try to court me yourself *before* now?"

"Because you're still vexed about the toad. Admittedly, I was not sure how exactly to woo you without being severely scolded."

I wanted to kiss him immensely for saying that. I did not because if there was any chance that somebody in the village was *not* at the ball, I did not want to damage our reputations even more. "I ought to return now then."

Evidently, it was not the response that Benjamin had expected. I did not get far from him before Benjamin grasped my hand. "Where do you think you are going? I am not finished."

"Well, I am. I'm going home, I said." I pulled my arm to no avail. "Release me, Ben."

Benjamin released me, but he stepped nearer to me, watching me closely. "You are running away."

How presumptuous! "I am not! I must have time to think about all of this."

"Oh, rubbish. You can think right here." Benjamin was challenging me. "I will let you out of this engagement, but only if you tell me that you do not love me the way that I love you."

He'd said the final part so casually that I wondered if he realised that he'd said it at all. Meanwhile, the words made my heart patter. I nearly admitted it, but I was already close to losing our battle of wits and it would not be done. I stepped back. "Good night, Mr. Blackburn."

He snatched my arm again. "Anna. Do you wish to be let off? Yes or no?"

"I DO NOT KNOW!" I cried.

"You do know. It is not a difficult question. Yes or no?"

It occurred to me that Benjamin would not relent. He was exhausted from this argument and so was I. "No," I said under my breath. Benjamin's shoulders fell. I had not realised how tense he was waiting for me to tell him that. "I surmise that the feelings of which you possess toward me are returned."

Benjamin laughed out loud and pulled me nearer. He used his thumb to lift my chin. "Then you failed."

The statement took me aback. I tried to relieve myself of his grip again, but not with much determination, if any. "I beg your pardon?"

"You've spent the last ten days trying to push me away. All you did was make me want you more." Benjamin smirked. "You failed."

"Fine." I smiled for the first time that night. "Let's go inform everybody then."

Benjamin was correct.

For, the scheme had not gone according to plan.

The End
12 Days Before Twelfth Night

ABOUT THE AUTHOR

Chloe is a student at Utah State University. She is majoring in Creative Writing and minoring in Folklore. She is the author of *Deceiving Mister Thornton* and *Beneath the Sycamore*. Chloe lives in Utah with her parents, two older brothers, her two angel doggies, Copper and Zoey, and her puppy, Rosetta.

instagram.com/authorchloekjames

A CHRISTMAS PROPOSAL

MADISON BAILEY

ALSO BY MADISON BAILEY

The Moore Family Series:

Hemiola

Unforgettable

CHAPTER 1

ANDREW

December 17, 1815
Castle Combe Village, Wiltshire, England

It was never a good sign when my father, the Baron of Castle Combe, summoned me to his study. Nearly all of our conversations took place there, him behind a heavy oak desk while I sat in the stiff velvet chair he'd arranged on the other side. Our visits always felt more like being called to the headmaster's office than a loving conversation between father and son.

Today, the clouds were thin in the gray sky, foretelling of a storm, but not the usual kind. The room was dim and stuffy, smelling of Father's cigar smoke.

"My Lord," I said as I stepped inside. Father put down his pen and looked up at me.

"Sit," he said, nodding at the chair. Father never wasted time with pleasantries, not with me, at least.

I walked across the room to the desk and rested my hand on the back of the chair, declining to obey his invitation. It was a small defiance, and yet it bolstered my confidence. I was taller than Father this way, and even though his stare still felt like a thousand icy daggers in my chest, I felt some level of power looking down on him.

"Unless you find an eligible lady to marry and settle down with her in three months' time, you will lose your inheritance and be cut off from this family." As soon as he was finished speaking, he picked up his quill pen and continued writing, as if he had only been commenting on the weather or the next time we would go hunting.

Father had made similar threats when I was younger, but as I was my parents' only living son, I knew they didn't carry much weight. I glanced at the family portrait that hung directly behind his desk, the last picture of our entire family. My older brother, Edward, had died soon after it was painted. To see him standing regally behind our mother, a subtle smile on his lips, was both a comfort and a painful reminder. I had idolized my brother and missed him every day. I was the first to admit Edward would have made a better baron, and Father never missed the opportunity to remind me he thought so too. Even if it was not explicitly stated, it was always implied. But much to everyone's chagrin, I was to inherit the barony.

"Father," I said, finally sitting down, crossing my ankle over my knee and resting my elbows on the armrests. "I'm old enough now to know how empty those threats are."

"That is where you are wrong. I have been in correspondence with a distant relation in America and it turns out that he is quite eligible to inherit our title and wealth. It is time you stop galivanting around bringing shame to the Fitzgerald name and the Castle Combe title. You are on thin ice, Andrew." He continued writing without looking up at me, still not deeming this conversation important enough to give his full attention to.

I thought describing my behavior as "bringing shame" to our family was a bit dramatic. I was boisterous, and had expensive taste, and loved dressing in bright colors my father thought were inappropriate for the future Baron of Castle Combe. But that was just the thing. I was the *future* Baron of Castle Combe, I wasn't a baron yet.

"Well, Father," I said, steepling my fingers and resting them on my mouth as a hasty idea formed in my mind. "I wasn't going to tell you this yet, but it just so happens that I have found a young woman I am interested in pursuing. In fact," I stopped to clear my throat and tried my very best to make this next lie convincing, "I was planning to propose to her for Christmas."

My father dropped his pen and finally refocused his attention on me. His eyes bore into mine as if he could see right through me. I wanted nothing more than to look away, but to do so would be all but admitting my fib.

"I don't believe you."

"That's fine, but I have invited her to Mother's Christmas house party. She'll be here in just a few days and you can see for yourself what an amiable match I am about to make."

Blast! I had just made this situation infinitely worse for myself. Mother's house party was set to begin in mere days. How was I going to find a woman who would be willing to act as my intended and sell the lie in a way that would be convincing enough to secure my inheritance? Why couldn't I simply conjure the perfect woman from thin air?

I looked at the family portrait again, my eyes drawn to Edward, as they always were. And that's when it hit me. *Langley.* My best mate from Oxford. He was so much like Edward, it was what had drawn me to him from the moment we met. And if I remembered correctly, he had a younger sister.

As I'd never before met Langley's sister, this was quite the risk. I didn't know if she was unattached—or even out in society, for that matter—but she was my best option. If I left at first light tomorrow morning, I could make it to Langley's home in

Nottinghamshire and we could return in time for the Christmas party. I could work out the rest of the details on the journey there and back.

It was a shaky plan, but it was a plan. At sunrise the next morning, I set my sights north, determined not to return home until I'd secured a willing co-conspirator.

CHAPTER 2

ELINOR

December 20, 1815
Nottinghamshire, England

I was, in my humble opinion, a very amiable young woman. I was the daughter of an Earl. I had a dowry of £25,000. I was a talented painter and could converse in English, French, and Italian. I could read Latin. My late Mama, may she rest in peace, had been meticulous in teaching me the rules and etiquette for a lady of my class and, on the whole, my behavior was becoming of a young woman and an honor to my family name. I was even moderately talented at the piano-forte. I had memorized two of Mozart's sonatas for the purpose of impressing others with the first one, obliging them for a second when they asked, and then feigning humility and allowing another lady to display her talents when they requested a third.

See, a perfect lady.

But were these strengths enough to recommend me despite the fact I was no longer in my very first season? Apparently not, because I was now returning to my family's country home heartbroken and very much *not* engaged.

I had been almost certain Lord Crane was going to ask for my hand and I had never been happier than at the thought of becoming his wife. But just days ago, when Lord Crane called and I was sure he was going to propose, he'd ended our courtship. And while the knife was fresh in my heart, he twisted it when he informed me he desired to pursue another young woman. She was the daughter of a viscount and her dowry was £5,000 less than mine, but it didn't matter because this Little Season had been her very first season out in society. And, for reasons I would never understand, that made her far more desirable than me. At least to Lord Crane.

I knew I shouldn't have let it affect me so much. If a man was going to choose another simply because she was a couple years younger and only in her first season, I should not waste tears on him. And yet, anytime I thought of Lord Crane, the corners of my eyes stung, and my throat felt as if I had swallowed a bite of potatoes without chewing them thoroughly enough.

"Elinor, darling," Charlotte, my beloved sister-in-law, said as we traveled home, "I know how disheartened you feel over Lord Crane, but you must look on the bright side. Now your children have no chance of inheriting noses far too large for their faces."

"I thought Lord Crane's prominent nose was charming." It came out half a laugh, half a sob, and I wiped at my eyes, embarrassed that she had caught me still feeling teary. Charlotte put down her embroidery and moved across the carriage to sit next to me. She put an arm around me and pulled me to her chest, resting her cheek on the top of my head.

My gaze settled on James, my older brother and the current Earl of Nottingham, who sat across from me, snoozing with his long legs spread as far as they could in the small carriage and his arms crossed over his chest. His soft snores were barely audible over the sound of the *clop-clop* of hooves and the creaking of the wheels over the path home.

"James and I both hope for someone far better than Lord Crane for you. Someone who loves you as much as you love him, who wants the best for you, who protects your heart. I was skeptical such men existed until I met your brother. But don't lose hope. He's out there for you."

"If you happen to see him, could you flag him down for me?" I teased, grateful Charlotte couldn't see the tear that escaped my eye and slid down my cheek.

"Who are we flagging down?" James asked, stirring at the sound of our voices, his voice still scratchy with sleep.

"Elinor's husband," Charlotte said.

"Oh, I wasn't aware you'd met someone while I was asleep," James said, one side of his mouth quirking up in a half-smile, half-smirk.

"It was his only opportunity to approach me, what with your attention diverted," I said, mirroring his same teasing expression.

James and I had lost our parents within three months of each other six years prior. With little extended family to rely on, he and I had forged an unbreakable bond in our grief. James was my safe harbor in the storm, and while I would always be grateful for the way he took care of me, I had become a tad frustrated by his overprotective nature as I entered society. I knew he meant well, but it was difficult to make connections with young men because he found far too many faults with any prospective match. That was one reason I had been so enamored with Lord Crane; not even my brother scared him.

When we arrived home a few hours later, we were surprised to see ours was not the only carriage in our drive.

"Were you expecting a visitor, love?" Charlotte asked James as he helped her out of the carriage.

"I wasn't." James helped me down from the carriage before taking long strides toward the house. "Is this the husband you were referring to?" he joked over his shoulder.

Before James had reached the large wooden door, it swung open, and a tall man walked out, his arms open wide as if it was his home we'd just arrived at. To say this man was handsome was a misuse of the English language. Every part of him, from his perfectly mussed, light brown hair and piercing gray eyes, to the peacock blue waistcoat that was perfectly tailored for his broad chest and shoulders, made me certain this man wasn't in fact real, but a hero who had escaped from the pages of a fairytale.

"Langley," the man boomed, "welcome home! I was beginning to fear I would need to send out a search party for you."

"Fitz, what are you doing here?" James said as he and the man embraced and slapped each other's backs in that odd, masculine way.

"I've come to invite you to my family's estate for Christmas."

"You couldn't have sent a letter for that?"

"*Well,*" our visitor drew out the single syllable, his voice pitching up an octave. "It's not just an invitation, I have something to request of your family. But before we get ahead of ourselves, you must introduce me to your lovely wife, and of course, your sister." I tried not to feel too disappointed that he hadn't referred to me as lovely too.

"Of course," James turned to us. "Fitz, this is Lady Charlotte Langley, my wife, and Lady Elinor, my sister. Charlotte, El, this is Mr. Andrew Fitzgerald, my closest friend."

"Ah, from your Oxford days," I said, managing to pull my eyes away from Mr. Fitzgerald. I'd heard many stories of their boyish antics at university, but I never imagined my brother's best friend was so easy to look at. I shook my head as if it would remove such thoughts from my head. He was probably married and here I was ogling him.

"A pleasure to meet you, Lady Elinor," Mr. Fitzgerald said, enveloping my hand in his and gently kissing my knuckles. There was the most wonderfully unsettling spinning in my stomach, and the sting of Lord Crane's rejection didn't feel nearly as painful anymore. "It is actually you specifically I must request something of."

I couldn't begin to imagine what he would need from me, but I already knew I would agree to anything this man asked of me.

"Shall we get out of the cold and go inside for this?" James pulled at his cravat and tilted his head back and forth. As he led Mr. Fitzgerald back inside, I noticed his shoulders tensed, weary of whatever his friend was going to ask of me.

We shed our warm cloaks and gloves in the entry way and entered the drawing room to find Mr. Fitzgerald had been there long enough to have a fire started and tea brought in. James and Charlotte sat on the sofa facing away from the window, close enough to each other for Charlotte to rest a comforting hand on her husband's knee. I settled into the sofa opposite them, facing the window and closest to the fire. Mr. Fitzgerald didn't sit at all. Instead, he paced back and forth in front of the fire. My eyes traced the veins webbed across the back of his hand until they disappeared into his sleeve.

"As you know," he began without any preamble, "I am a perpetual disappointment to my father. And apparently it has gone to the point where he is willing to disinherit me and pass the barony to a wretched, distant American cousin if I don't shape up and settle down."

Ah, so he wasn't married.

"So, I was thinking," Mr. Fitzgerald continued. "Perhaps

the three of you could come to my family's Christmas house party and Lady Elinor could pretend to be my betrothed. Or at least my intended."

"Of course," I said at the same time James said, "Absolutely not."

"Elinor, you cannot be serious." James leveled me with the same gaze that had deterred many men who had tried to develop a connection with me over the course of two Seasons and two Little Seasons. Luckily, I could give it right back.

"What's the harm?" I shrugged. I knew the response had been a result of a heart that was too often louder than my head. But the thought of the Christmas party sparked hope, a feeling that had been in short supply since Lord Crane's rejection.

"For starters, your reputation," James put his index finger out as if prepared to list off a myriad of reasons. "A broken engagement is not something that you want in your past if you hope to make a suitable match."

"You will recall that Lord Crane did not deem me a suitable match, and that was without a broken engagement."

"Come now, love, it's 1815. I don't think a broken engagement is as bad a blight as it used to be, especially if it is Elinor who breaks off the courtship," Charlotte said in her soothing way. It was the only thing I'd ever seen that had been able to calm my brother.

"Whose side are you on?" James turned to face his wife.

Before Charlotte could respond, I said, "Perhaps a visit to Mr. Fitzgerald's family estate for the holidays is the perfect balm for the humiliation that this past Little Season turned out to be."

"I promise you, Langley, Elinor – can I call you Elinor?"

"No." James folded his arms and leveled Mr. Fitzgerald with the most firey gaze. Apparently using my Christian name so soon after suggesting I pretend to be his betrothed was too much for my brother.

"Brother, it is my name. Shouldn't I be the one to decide who gets to use it?" I turned my attention to Mr. Fitzgerald. "Yes, you may call me Elinor."

"Elinor," he drew out each syllable in my name, his intoxicating eyes locked on mine the entire time, like my name was a sweet he was savoring, "will escape this house party with her reputation intact."

Breaking eye contact with Mr. Fitzgerald, I chanced a quick look at James. His eyes were narrowed at me, and he fidgeted with Papa's ring on his pinky finger. I knew I was in for a stern talking to once we were in private.

Mr. Fitzgerald, however, did not seem to notice James' discomfort. Or if he did, he didn't mind. He continued, "The blame for our broken engagement will be laid wholly at my feet. All of the *ton* will know that the young Lady Langley is an upstanding woman and that I was a fool for letting her get away."

"What is the point of this ruse if, after the holidays, you are right back where you started? Wifeless and without any intentions to marry. Is this boneheaded plan not just delaying your inevitable disinheritance?" James stood now too, going around the sofa and leaned against it, his arms propping him up.

"I am hoping that if my father sees that I have the potential to court a respectable young woman, he'll hold out hope a little longer for me."

"That is highly questionable," James pushed himself off the back of the sofa and began pacing behind it.

As I tracked his walk back and forth, I saw storm clouds rolling in and noticed they were the same color as Mr. Fitzgerald's eyes. Perhaps I should have taken that as a bad omen, an impending emotional storm, but inclement weather had never deterred me before, and it wasn't going to now.

"Give me some credit, Langley," Mr. Fitzgerald said, pressing his hand to his chest in an overexaggerated gesture of mock offense. "You're my oldest friend."

"And it is exactly because I know you better than anyone else that I am vehemently opposed to this ill-thought-out ruse. Going to duel? I'll be your second. Killed a man? I'm sure you had good reason, let me grab my shovel. But Elinor, and anything involving Elinor, is a line I will not cross, not even for you."

"Ahem," I cleared my throat and both men turned their attention to me. "As I will play a key part in this plan, I think my opinion should be heard. And not just heard, deferred to."

"As your guardian, my opinion overrules yours."

"I'm twenty years old, Brother. I can make my own decisions. And besides, it's not some stranger asking this of us. It's Andrew – may I call you Andrew?" I said, turning to him, a half a smirk on my lips as I mirrored both Andrew's words and intonation in asking that important question. It felt too intimate to use a man's Christian name when I'd only met him moments ago, but I found I liked it. I also liked the extreme distress my brother appeared to be in at my use of it. He looked at me, his lips pressed into a firm line, an expression in his eyes that said *I cannot believe you just said that.*

"He's your best friend," I pressed on. "And he may be part of the equation, but so am I. Do you not trust me to be wise? You are, after all, not the only one with hopes for my future."

James began pacing again, one hand behind his neck, filling his cheeks with a deep inhale.

Charlotte turned, folding her arms over the back of the sofa and leaning her chin on them. "It could be fun, love."

James stopped, pinning her with a stare that might start

anyone else on fire. "Elinor pretending to be my best friend's betrothed would be *fun*?"

"No, not that part." I couldn't see her face, as she was turned away from me, but her tone sounded as if she was rolling her eyes. "Going away for Christmas. Mingling with others, making new friends. It could be refreshing."

Andrew smacked his hands together, startling me. "Langley, are you really going to deny your wife the pleasure of visiting Castle Combe for Christmas? She's going to love it."

James scrubbed his jaw, looking between Charlotte, me, and Andrew before letting out a long sigh. "El, you must absolutely promise me you will not fall in love with him." He pointed an accusing finger at Andrew.

Making such a promise could very well make a liar out of me, but I drew a cross over my heart and said, "I solemnly swear I will not fall in love with him."

He sighed, dropping his chin to his chest, pinching the bridge of his nose. "Fine. We can go."

Despite the fact I knew this engagement was a complete farce, my heart leapt as if James had just given Andrew approval to actually marry me. I felt slightly lightheaded with the excitement of the house party and to be close to Andrew in the coming days, to be the focus of his attention and to be near enough to memorize all of him.

"Splendid!" Andrew said, his huge smile lighting his face. "I knew you'd come around."

"But you must promise me, both of you," James said, rounding the sofa, "neither of you will do anything to put Elinor's reputation in jeopardy."

"It's the season of giving," I said, standing up and smoothing out my skirt, "so give us – or me at the very least – a little credit."

Andrew's eyes met mine and I could have sworn that the look we shared buzzed with an energy unlike anything I'd ever shared with another person. Even Lord Crane. I thanked the heavens my dress was long-sleeved so he could not see the thousands of goosebumps that spread up my arms. My head was adamant that this would not solve my heartbreak over Lord Crane. In fact, it would probably only add to it. But my heart replied that it would be a future Elinor problem. Andrew Fitzgerald was going to be the most wonderful distraction.

CHAPTER 3

ANDREW

December 23, 1815
Castle Combe Village, Wiltshire, England

I was not prepared for how beautiful Langley's sister was. Her hair was the color of shimmering fields of wheat. I longed to run my fingers through it to find out if it was as silky as it looked. Her deep brown eyes hinted at an underlying mischievousness, and I was struck by how unlike her older brother she was. Where Langley was stoic and a staunch follower of the rules, Elinor was expressive and exhibited a side of subtle rebelliousness.

And her name. *Elinor.* It was so perfect for her. I knew I was taking quite the risk to request the liberty of calling her by her Christian name after knowing her for mere minutes. But if I was going to ask her to fake an engagement with me, surely we were afforded a few intimacies to help us sell the lie.

I would have liked to use the journey back to Castle Combe to get to learn more of Elinor and get our stories straight, but Langley had insisted we travel back in my carriage, while Lady Langley and Elinor traveled behind us in theirs. His insistence was probably for the better, if I was being honest with myself. Since I'd met her three days earlier, Elinor had permeated all my thoughts, and I was beginning to seriously doubt my plan. Was my inheritance worth securing if I lost my heart in the process? During the hours we traveled to Castle Combe, I even began to wonder if Elinor and I could develop a relationship founded on real feelings. Was there a chance she might consider becoming my baroness?

I glanced across the carriage and knew I needed to nip such thoughts in the bud. Aside from the fact that Langley would skin me alive if I fell in love with his sister, I had my own reasons for my perpetual bachelorhood and I wouldn't create disaster just because Elinor was beautiful and intriguing.

As we arrived at Castle Combe, I found myself wishing I could watch her face as she saw it for the first time. I had complicated emotions about my childhood home, but what would someone who had never been here think of it? Fat, fluffy snowflakes began falling as we arrived in the village and I looked out the window, trying to see my home with new eyes.

I suppose one who had never visited would say Castle Combe was reminiscent of a story book village, covered in sparkling, white snow. Each stone house had a bright painted front door, their brown facades decorated with greenery and ribbons for the coming Christmas holiday. The windows glowed from the fires inside, cozy on this overcast winter day.

Soon we crested a hill and Castle Combe Manor came into view. Built in classic, English country home style, the manor was somehow both grandiose and cozy. It was built from the same tan bricks the homes in the village were made of. Snow covered the many pointed gables and carved stonework adorning the roof, and smoke floated lazily from each of the oversized chimneys. Vines twisted their way over the stone walls, bare of their leaves.

As we pulled up to the manor, my stomach clenched at the

sight of the three figures waiting for us on the steps. I was happy to see my mother and grandmother, but the sight of my father made me feel like I wanted to tell the driver to just keep going.

The carriage finally stopped and the footman opened the door, but Langley put a hand on my arm, stopping me before I could step out.

"Elinor will leave here in two weeks with both her heart and her reputation intact," he said, his eyes boring into mine. "We're clear on that, aren't we?"

I wanted to laugh it off and make a witty comment, but feeling my father's eyes on me filled me with dread. "Believe me, I want this to be over with just as much as you do."

We walked to the other carriage and Langley helped his wife out before stepping out of the way so I could help Elinor out. She took my outstretched hand, and warmth spread from my hand, filling my whole body. My gaze stayed on our hands, imagining how wonderful it would be to feel her skin on mine, uninhibited by our gloves.

She reached up and rubbed her thumb between my eyebrows. "You're scowling," she said concern creasing her own forehead. Her voice and her touch were comforting, and suddenly, facing my father didn't seem like such a feat.

"Yes, just a little nervous," I said, weaving her hand through my arm. "I have no doubt my mother and grand-mother will love you. My father is a different story, but don't take it personally. I'm not sure he likes anyone."

As we walked closer to the house, I leaned close to Elinor's ear and whispered, "I feel much more confident having you by my side." Her hair smelled like roses and as she turned to reply, I was captivated by the honey-colored streaks in her dark eyes.

"I'm glad to be a support for you," she said, smiling. "At least until you can find your real wife." She winked at me before refocusing her attention on my family on the steps.

Introducing Elinor to my family went exactly as I predicted it would. Mother gave both of us a rib-crushing hug, Gammie cut me off in the middle of trying to introduce her with her full title to insist that Elinor call her "Gammie" just like everyone else, and Father was cordial enough to say, "Welcome to our home," in the most unwelcoming tone before turning to walk back inside.

As we stood in the foyer, a small white Pomeranian rushed down the hall towards us and began yipping and hopping around our feet.

"Who is this?" I asked, scooping the fluffy bundle up and holding him to my eye level. His pink tongue out, each hot breath he panted warmed my cool nose. When I'd departed Castle Combe three days earlier, we definitely did not have a small dog.

"Oh, this is Dash," Gammie said, reaching up to pet his head.

"One of our tenants was returning to London and didn't want to take their newly acquired pet with them," Mother said. "So now he is *our* newly acquired pet. You know how your grandmother is. She can't turn away anyone or anything in need of help."

"I must admit, this is one of your cuter charity cases, Gammie," I said, handing the squirming puppy to her.

"I agree," Gammie said, planting kisses on the dog's nose and between his eyes. "But be sure not to let him outside without a lead. We were out together yesterday and he was almost snatched up by a buzzard."

I highly doubted such a story, but agreed to be careful anyway.

As the men joined the women in the drawing room after dinner that evening, I immediately began searching for Elinor and found her warming her hands near the large stone fireplace, her back to me. Not long after we arrived, the other house party guests began arriving and my attentions that afternoon had been on greeting them with my parents. I was hoping that this evening would give me more time to spend with Elinor. If we were going to make this fake courtship convincing, we were going to need more than a few moments here and there in each other's presence. She turned around as I walked towards her and smiled when she noticed me. Pride bubbled inside of me to be the reason for her smile.

"Andrew," Gammie said, demanding everyone's attention. "You must tell us the story of how you met Lady Langley and how you proposed."

"Oh no, I'm sure no one wants to hear that," I said with a cough, my eyes darting to Elinor, silently begging her to say something, anything, to get Gammie to drop the subject.

"Yes, dear, I love so much when you tell the story." The smile that curled one corner of her mouth let me know she had indeed understood my desperate look and had deliberately chosen to ignore it.

I returned her mischievous gaze and shook my head. As Langley had made certain Elinor and I had practically no time to discuss what kind of story would be told to keep up our ruse, I knew I was going to have to think fast. "Alright, fine." I cleared my throat and faced the room.

"I met Lady Elinor at Lady Crowley's ball. I knew immediately that I wanted to court her, but there were quite a few things in my way."

"My brother, first of all," she interjected. "But perhaps the bigger obstacle was Mr. Fitzgerald's complete ineptitude at wooing a young woman. During his first visit, he did not come bearing flowers or even a love poem, but a small pigeon."

"Good heavens," Mother gasped, "Andrew, was it alive?"

"It was quite dead," Elinor said dryly.

My eyes snapped to hers. Was she being quite serious? We had agreed that this ruse would keep her reputable, but did that mean she had to completely decimate *my* reputation in the process? Fine. If this is how she wanted to do this, I would match her, blow for blow.

"It was in reference to a conversation we'd had during our first dance," I said, taking over the storytelling. "In an attempt to compliment the color of my eyes, which she found captivating," – she rolled her eyes at this, but I continued – "she said they were the color of a pigeon she'd seen that morning."

"And it was during that same conversation Mr. Fitzgerald compared my eyes to those of a toad."

Gammie's mouth fell open and I stifled a laugh, digging deep for a witty reply.

"What can I say, the lighting in the ballroom was terrible. But never mind that because the next day, I invited her to promenade in Hyde Park where I was able to ascertain that the color of her eyes is more closely compared to mud, not a toad."

The guests audibly gasped, the expressions on their faces ranging from disgust to amusement.

"But to Mr. Fitzgerald's great credit, he found a much better way to describe the color of my eyes and he brought me a beautiful bouquet of flowers. Unfortunately, he is allergic, and we could hardly have more than a few words back and forth before he would devolve into a sneezing fit."

"Allergies aside, I must not have been that terrible at wooing you because you did accept my proposal."

"Ah yes, just a few weeks into our courtship, he arrived at my home to propose bearing a toad."

"Please tell me it was alive this time?" Mother asked, her eyes closed, pinching the bridge of her nose.

"Alive and well," Elinor said, "I've named him Reginald

and grown quite fond of him. So, my dear Mr. Fitzgerald comes in, gets down on one knee."

"Dearest," I said, "I think you're remembering incorrectly. I was standing, like a gentleman."

"And a single tear slid down his cheek," she reached out and traced a tear down the edge of my face, not even bothering to acknowledge my interjection. "And he offered me the toad and said—"

"'Lady Langley, will you marry me?' And she said 'Yes.' The end." Our eyes met, like she was silently scolding me for ruining her fun, but I feared that if I didn't bring the story to a close, I was going to lose all respectability.

It was clear our audience didn't know how to react to our story. Some of them smiled and said a proposal story filled with inside jokes was sweet, others just shook their heads in disbelief. I knew the story was a bit of a stretch if we were trying to convince the others that we were a real couple, but found joy in sharing the ridiculousness with Elinor. I could see out of the corner of my eye that she was doing her best to keep her composure. I kept my sights forward, because I knew if I looked at her, we would both be struck with a fit of laughter.

"Well," Gammie cleared her throat and took a sip of tea. "That is quite the story."

"What can I say?" I said, finally looking at Elinor. It was a miracle I was able to stifle the laugh, but couldn't hold back the huge smile. "Lady Elinor is quite the woman."

CHAPTER 4

ELINOR

December 24, 1815

Despite our long travel days and staying up late playing games in the drawing room last night, I awoke just as dawn was breaking the next morning. It was Christmas Eve, and I knew as soon as the rest of the house was awake, we would be swept up in Christmas traditions; gathering greenery, hanging the kissing bough, finding a yule log.

I paced back and forth in front of the embers of last night's fire, but it wasn't enough. I needed some crisp morning air and a longer walk to clear my head.

I slipped on my boots and wrapped myself in my cloak, buttoning it under my chin. James would have a fit if he knew I was leaving my room in my nightgown, but I didn't have time to ring for my maid to help me get dressed properly. And besides, the heavy winter cloak provided ample modesty and it was unlikely I would see any of my fellow guests on a brisk morning stroll.

I went down the stairs, wincing when a few of the steps creaked, and out the front door. I could see from my room a quaint winter garden I thought would provide the perfect place to walk and think.

You must absolutely promise me you will not fall in love with him. James' words from days earlier still rang in my ears. Didn't he know me well enough to know that if anyone told me *not* to do something, I was likely to do that very thing out of spite? Perhaps James should have chosen a best friend that wasn't quite so easy to fall in love with. The thought stopped me in the path. Surely I wasn't actually *in love* with Andrew, not after only knowing him a few days. Not after feeling so humiliated and hurt over Lord Crane.

But here I was, already using Andrew's Christian name. Already looking forward to seeing him this morning, already hoping that as we all gathered greenery and went in search of a yule log, that Andrew and I would have a moment alone to share conversation no one else could hear, to tease each other as we had last night when Gammie asked about how he had proposed.

I began walking again, so lost in my own thoughts I didn't notice until I made it to the winter garden that Dash had followed me out of the manor. He bounced joyfully ahead of me in the snow.

"Dash!" I called after him, worried he would get too far ahead of me and I would lose him.

Suddenly, I heard the squawk of a buzzard and watched in horror as he swooped down, snatching Dash in his talons and taking flight. I thought Gammie had only been joking when she'd warned us about letting Dash outside without a lead.

My heard sped up and I took off running, yelling at the bird to drop Dash and flailing my arms around in hopes I would appear more threatening than I felt. I stopped only long enough to take off my boot, flinging it at the buzzard, praying it wouldn't hit the dog. It had the intended effect and the bird let go of Dash. But I had not accounted for how high he had already flown and how far the small, white puppy had to fall. I pumped my legs, determined to catch him before he would hit the ground, fearing I would be too late.

I flung myself forward, slipping in the snow, and landing in a giant puddle of freezing water and mud, but breathing a sigh of relief when I caught Dash. He rewarded me for saving his life by licking my cold cheeks.

I stood up, still gripping the dog and brushing off my cloak as if anything I could do would make the sight of me – soaking wet, shivering, and muddy – better. To make matters worse, I was down a boot and losing feeling in my exposed foot quickly.

"Elinor?" I heard Andrew's raspy voice behind me and cursed under my breath.

"A buzzard was attempting to steal the dog," I said by way of explanation, turning to face him.

Andrew looked me up and down before bursting out in laughter, the joyous sound echoing in the crisp morning air.

"And," I pulled up the hem of my nightgown to show him my soiled stocking, "I sacrificed my shoe to save him."

I'm not sure what I was expecting him to do, but it certainly wasn't what he did next. Still laughing, he walked towards me and scooped me up, one arm behind my back, the other behind my knees, Dash nestled on my stomach, oblivious to the butterflies that fluttered there.

"We can get you new boots. Let's get you inside before you freeze," he said, his warm breath tickling my cheek.

"I am capable of walking, you know," I said, slightly breathless.

"I know, but that would ruin your stockings further."

Oh yes, surely this was completely about saving my stockings. And even though I could have called his bluff and demanded he put me down, I found I was quite enjoying the present situation. His arms were sure and confident, and I resisted the urge to reach up and feel the dark stubble that he hadn't shaved away yet. My eyes studied the bow in his top lip, and the steady rise and fall of his chest calmed my shivering. I could feel his heartbeat beneath where my hand rested on his neck.

"What are you doing out this early anyway?" he asked.

I was hoping the cold air would clear my head of you, I thought. But instead I said, "I just wanted a quick morning walk. I didn't know Dash snuck out behind me." At the sound of his name, the now-muddy Pomeranian lifted his head, the tip of his tongue out as he panted so it looked like he was smiling.

Andrew turned and used his back to push open the heavy wood front doors, walking us backwards into the entryway. As he spun us to face forward again, we found James coming down the stairs, one hand on the ornately carved railing. His eyes immediately landed on Andrew's arm around my back.

"What's this?" James asked, one eyebrow raised.

"Turns out Gammie was right, buzzards are hunting Pomeranians nowadays," Andrew said casually, setting me down.

"I lost my boot and fell in a puddle trying to rescue the dog," I said, "and Andrew was just making sure I didn't ruin my stockings further or get a frostbitten foot."

"Hm," James hummed, looking between us, taking in our muddle, disheveled appearances.

"I'll take Dash and see if Gammie's maid can give him a bath." Andrew said, clearing his throat and taking the dog from me. "And I'll see you both at breakfast."

I watched him walk down the hall towards the back of the manor, admiring the way his coat stretched across his back, almost losing myself in the moments-old memory of being in those muscular arms.

"Oh my goodness," James said, pulling my attention back

to him. "You're developing feelings for him. I can see it in your face."

"Don't worry," I said, gathering a handful of my heavy, wet cloak in my fists so I could walk up the stairs. "I don't have feelings for him. But one cannot resist admiring a man when he is built like a Greek god."

"For the love of all that is holy, please do not refer to Fitz as a Greek god, and please do your best not to admire him." James looked at the ceiling as if pleading for heavenly help and blew out a long breath.

I stopped on the step James was still standing on and turned to face him squarely. "Help me understand something, Brother. Why would it be such a bad thing if we did develop feelings for one another? Andrew is your best friend and I can't imagine you would be friends with a terrible person."

"I don't think he's terrible. It's just that he's –" James stopped, biting his lip as he tried to find the right words. "He's non-committal, a perpetual bachelor. I'm not sure he's capable of being serious about anything. He wouldn't mean to break your heart, but he would break it nonetheless. I know how much you want a love like Mother and Fathers. I have found that with Charlotte, and I can attest to how utterly wonderful it is." He smiled as he spoke of his wife. "I want it for you too. But Fitz isn't the man that's going to give that to you."

What if the reason Andrew wasn't married yet was because he hadn't found the right woman and not because he was incapable of being serious? And what if I was the right woman for him? Having just denied that I had any feelings for Andrew, I knew I couldn't voice these questions to James.

"You mustn't worry so much about me," I said, giving him a reassuring smile.

"I will always worry about you."

"I know, but I will be careful. I am not eager for another broken heart."

I listened to the clip of James' shoes as he walked to the breakfast room and continued up the stairs to change out of my wet clothes, fearing that if my brother was right about Andrew, I was already barreling towards heartache, no matter how magnetic it felt when we were together.

CHAPTER 5

ANDREW

December 24, 1815

The day had been spent out of doors gathering the greenery and holly to decorate the manor for Christmas. We were in the drawing room, warming up with cups of hot cider and sucking on peppermint sticks. Candles lit the room in a warm glow and the air was filled with the luxurious scent of pine. Dash raced around our feet, unscathed from his brush with death that morning.

All the couples were taking turns kissing beneath the mistletoe and I was surprised to see even Father pulled Mother beneath the leaves and planted a chaste kiss on her mouth. It was the most human thing I'd ever seen the man do.

"Andrew, it's your turn!" Gammie called from across the room.

"Oh, no," Elinor said, her eyes darting quickly to my mouth and then back to Gammie. "We aren't married yet, it would be improper."

"When you get to be my age, you realize that propriety is

absolute nonsense. You're young, you're in love. It's Christmas."

I looked at Elinor and she lifted her shoulder in a small shrug as if to say, *Why not?*

Langley and his wife were sitting on the settee and even from across the room, I could see his jaw clenched so firmly I was sure he had broken one of his molars. Lady Langley placed a hand on her husband's arm. If she hadn't, I was certain he would have leapt across the room to rip me to shreds.

Even knowing that my best friend would hate me for it, I had definitely *thought* about kissing Elinor, but it was not like this, surrounded by people and my parents and my geriatric grandmother. I knew kissing her would destroy the dam I had spent my whole life building around my heart, but figured a quick peck beneath the mistletoe would satisfy Gammie and only cause a small crack in the dam, not complete destruction.

I slipped my hand in Elinor's and lead her to where the mistletoe was hung. I made a concerted effort not to look her in her gorgeous dark eyes, but it didn't help to focus on any other feature of her face because every single one was just as beautiful. My gaze dropped to her collarbone, highlighted in the candlelight. Bad idea. Every part of her ignited something in me: the desire to learn how every inch of her porcelain skin felt on my mouth. I wished I could order everyone out of the room so we could have this moment just her and me.

I took a deep breath and allowed my lips to touch Elinor's for only a fraction of a second. "There you go, Gammie."

"Andrew," she scolded me. "Kiss her like you mean it."

I would never recover from what I was about to do. And I'm not saying my reputation would never recover. My heart would never recover. Was this worth it? Should I admit Elinor and I weren't truly engaged and get us out of this?

I refocused my attention on Elinor, finally allowing myself to look her in the eye.

"It's okay," she whispered. The words broke the dam before I'd even had a chance to truly know the exact shape of her lips beneath mine.

My hands went to her neck, cradling her face and tracing her smooth jawline with my thumb. Time and space seemed to bow to my will as I took in every precious second before I jumped over the edge and shattered the world as I knew it. Even before I kissed her, I knew my life would be defined by two eras: before Elinor Langley and after her.

There was nothing slow or tentative about the way Elinor's lips parted for mine. She tasted like spiced cider and her skin smelled like home. Not the manor or our London house in Mayfair, but a place where I was loved simply because I existed. Her hands went to my waist and pulled me toward her, her body fitting perfectly against mine. I turned my head to deepen our kiss, keeping one hand on her neck and wrapping my other arm around the small of her back. She wrapped her arms around my neck, her fingers tangled in my hair.

With every ounce of willpower I possessed, I pulled my mouth away from hers, but I kept her pressed close to me. Our eyes locked and everyone else faded away.

"Whoa," she said, her voice barely audible. I almost thought I had imagined it.

"Now *that* is a kiss," Gammie said, clasping her hands over her heart.

I finally let go of Elinor, and despite trying to look anywhere else, my gaze landed on Langley. *Way too far,* his eyes seemed to scream at me from across the room. I shrugged, hoping the gesture assured him that the kiss was only to keep up the appearance of our courtship. It didn't look like he believed me, but I couldn't blame him because while everyone went on with their Christmas Eve celebrations, I grappled with the realization that my heart was no longer mine. It now beat outside my chest.

CHAPTER 6

ELINOR

December 24, 1815

The harder I tried to *not* think about our mistletoe kiss – Andrew's smooth lips on mine, the taste of the peppermint stick he'd been eating, the smell of the fresh winter greenery we'd just brought in to decorate with, his arm wrapped protectively around my waist, holding me against him – the warmer my room seemed to become. And if I allowed my thoughts to settle on the most glorious moment of my young life, my heart began to beat so quickly that I knew I could never find sleep in this state.

I buried my face in my pillow, trying desperately to think of all the worst things, but it was no use. Not only had Andrew overtaken my heart, he had well and fully taken over my mind.

After what felt like hours trying to rest, I sat up, gathering my hair and holding it at the top of my head in an effort to find coolness and comfort. I filled my cheeks with the biggest breath I could, exhaling as loud as I dared in the darkness. I couldn't stay in this room a moment longer.

I threw a shawl around my nightdress and lit a candle from the dying fire in the grate before slipping from my room. While I wasn't entirely confident I could find my way to the library in the darkness, I set off in that direction. The only thing, I knew, that would lull me to sleep was perhaps a volume on the husbandry of ducks or how to properly ride side saddle. And I was determined to find the largest and most boring tome I could.

I cracked open a door to what I believed was the library and was relieved to see I was in the right place. The fire had not gone out in the hearth, its warm glow dancing over all the leather volumes. I stepped in all the way, turning my back to the room to shut the door as soundlessly as possible.

"You can't sleep either, huh?"

I slapped my hand over my mouth to stifle a startled cry and nearly dropped my candle stick as I turned around to find Andrew sprawled out on the rug in front of the fireplace, his hands behind his head.

"Good heavens, you startled me!"

"Sorry." He didn't sound remotely apologetic.

"I have come to find the most boring book your family owns."

"Hmm, I believe on that shelf over there," he craned his neck and pointed to the far corner of the room, "is where Father stores the ledgers my grandfather kept for the estate. They were taking up too much room in his study. They might be just the thing you're looking for. There is also a dictionary somewhere in here, if you'd prefer that."

The original plan had been to retrieve a book and return to my room quickly, but that didn't seem so pressing anymore. I walked along the edge of the room, lifting the candlelight closer to the shelves so I could read the spines. "Why are you on the floor?" I asked.

"It's warmer down here, next to the fire. If I can't sleep, the heat usually helps."

"Does sleep evade you often?"

"It does when I'm home."

I abandoned the appearance of looking for a book and walked over to Andrew, perching myself on the sofa and setting my candle on the side table. I pulled my shawl tighter around my shoulders and leaned forward, resting my elbow on my knee, my chin in my hand.

"Do you not enjoy the manor?" I asked. "It seems so idyllic here."

"I love my mother. And Gammie. I come home mostly for them."

It was impossible to miss that he hadn't affirmed that he liked the manor itself. And the omission of his father in the list of people he returned home for loomed even greater.

We didn't say anything for a moment, the only sound in the room was the crackling of the logs in the hearth. Perhaps it was the soft glow of the fire, or the late hour, or the storm of emotions I was trying to wade through, but instead of staying at the very appropriate distance and the very safe seated position on the sofa, I moved to the ground, laying down next to Andrew, my hands on my stomach as I stared up at the ceiling. It, like the rest of the manor, was adorned with beautiful millwork.

Andrew didn't seem surprised by my move to the floor, nor did he attempt to put any distance between us. He removed his hands from behind his head, resting his arms at his sides. We were not touching, but only a breath apart. Out of my peripheral vision, I could see the rise and fall of his broad chest.

"May I ask you something?" I said. As much as I wanted to, I was terrified to turn my neck to face him. To be this close to his mouth again and keep my gaze on his eyes instead would take every ounce of willpower I possessed. While I was trying my best not to make it ridiculously obvious how deep my feelings for Andrew had become, I was certain the deception was failing. And to give him this close a direct gaze in my eyes would ruin any plausible deniability I had left.

"Of course." He turned to look at me.

"With your inheritance on the line, why didn't you just find an actual wife? I cannot imagine that you, being who you are, would have a hard time finding a most willing woman."

He turned his gaze back to the ceiling. "I'm not sure I'll ever get married."

"Because you don't want to?"

"Because I am half my father."

I finally broke my resolve to keep my gaze anywhere but on him. His Adam's apple bobbed in his throat as he swallowed. "What do you mean?"

"I'm sure you've been able to tell these past days, my father is not the most nurturing of creatures. And that's putting it nicer than he deserves. I am not the first-born son, I was never meant to inherit the barony. I know how disappointed he is that he must pass the barony to me. I feel it every day. And all of that might be bearable if I knew that he could at least love my mother, but even she had a role to play, and having fulfilled it, is no longer a priority to him."

He paused for a moment, but I could sense he wasn't done, so I stayed quiet, hoping the silence would encourage him to go on.

"Mother insists he wasn't always like this, that at one point in their relationship, there was love there, but I have the hardest time imaging that. I sometimes wonder if she loves him too much, and it has always been unrequited. And should I ever marry, I cannot decide what is worse: being the one who is incapable of returning love, or being the one for whom the love is not returned. The simple answer seems to be to avoid it altogether."

"But if you don't have an heir, the barony passes to that American cousin anyway, does it not?"

"At that point, I'll be dead and gone and I don't care who, if anyone, inherits it after me. I want the means to live comfortably and be generous to the tenants of Castle Combe. And once I am the Baron, perhaps I can adopt one of their sons and bequeath the whole thing to him. The fact remains that I will do the least damage to another human being if I remain a bachelor."

"You mustn't forget you are half your mother as well. And I would argue you are far more like her than you are your father. All the best parts of you, you got from her."

"That is true," Andrew said, lifting his shoulders in a shrug, "but even if I am more like my mother, do I have the potential to become as unfeeling as my father because there are parts of him in me too?"

"I think a great deal of that is up to you. You can always choose to be a better man than he is. You can choose to marry someone you actually love, and to see them as a human being, and not just as an object to satisfy a role you cannot fill on your own."

"Hm, I've never thought about it like that before."

We laid in silence for a bit, and I wondered if I should return to my room. But to leave would mean that another one of our limited number of moments would be over. And as Andrew had just admitted that he would never marry, affirming what James had told me, my heart was torn in two directions.

I had known, of course, when I agreed to this plan, that the ruse would end in a fortnight. And while I was positive the pull between us wasn't just a figment of my imagination, it seemed that even if our feelings for each other were becoming real, it wasn't going to change his decision about getting married. But now I knew the feeling of his arms around me, of his lips on mine. And that knowledge was a fire that I feared was going to consume me for the rest of my life.

"When I came to invite you to the house party, you mentioned a Lord Crane and that your Little Season had not gone well. What happened?" Andrew asked me, his voice soft.

Lord Crane had not crossed my mind a single time since we had arrived in Castle Combe and it felt strange to me that I had once felt heartbroken over his rejection. Surely it was more of the *idea* of marriage to him that I was mourning.

"I was, or at least I believed I was, about to be engaged, but Lord Crane informed me that he was going to propose to another because she had only been out in society for one season."

Andrew whipped his head to look at me so quickly I feared he would break his neck. "You cannot be serious." His eyes were wide.

I turned my head to face him too and giggled. "I am. And I thought it was one of the hardest rejections I would ever face. The night he told me, I think I laid awake all night wondering *why*, infusing meaning into all our conversations, especially into our last one. And I have feared ever since then that no matter my dowry or my talents or my accomplishments, maybe I am just not beautiful enough to stand a chance against the other young ladies of the *ton*. In a world so focused on how everything looks, it seems nothing else matters." I moved my hand from my stomach to my side and felt the edge of my pinky brush up against Andrew's.

"And I fear that means *I* don't matter," I whispered, voicing the one nagging thought that had plagued me since my very first season out in society.

Andrew's hand moved over mine, intertwining our fingers. His thumb tracing the edge of mine, up and down.

"Elinor," he said.

"Hm?"

"You are a very," he paused, and I held my breath, "*very* beautiful woman."

I thought for a moment that gravity no longer had any hold on me, and I knew that for as long as I could breathe, my heart would beat for Andrew.

CHAPTER 7

ELINOR

January 3, 1816

Christmas Eve was not the last time Andrew and I met in the library after everyone was in bed. In fact, sleep evaded me every night after that one. Perhaps it was because I wasn't in my own bed, but I think the more likely reason was because I was falling in love.

In those quiet hours, Andrew told me about his older brother, Edward. I told him about my parents, and how the holidays made me miss them even more. We talked about lighter things too, about Andrew's favorite places to take morning rides on his favorite horse, about my favorite books and how I hoped to paint the idyllic scenery of Castle Combe, perhaps in the summer when it was much more enjoyable to be outside.

The daylight did not dim my desire to be near Andrew and I was glad that our ruse required me to be on his arm often.

As we drew closer to the end of the house party, I knew I needed to be honest about my feelings. To both my brother and to Andrew. Somehow, being honest with Andrew seemed far less scary.

I wasn't sure there was ever going to be a good time to tell James that I had gone against his admonition not to fall in love with his best friend, but it certainly wasn't in the middle of the night while I was leaving my room to meet Andrew in the library.

I was just slipping quietly out of my room, pinching my cheeks to give my complexion a little color, when James cleared his throat behind me. "Where are you going?"

I spun around, hands on my chest. "You scared me," I whispered.

"We need to talk," James whispered fiercely back, pointing towards my room. "And Charlotte is already asleep, so we'll need to use your room."

I nodded, reaching behind me, opening the door again, and stepping into my room.

"You didn't answer my question," James said, his voice still only slightly above a whisper when we had shut the bedroom door behind us.

"I can't sleep, I was going to the library for a book."

"So you haven't been able to sleep every night, is that right?"

"No, just tonight."

"You do know sound travels in this house, right?" James paced in front of the hearth, scrubbing his jaw. "I have heard you leaving your room every night. And not returning until hours later."

Caught in my lie, I decided the best course of action was to remain silent and let my brother do the talking.

"And when we were in school, Fitz was a chronic insomniac and preferred to spend the nighttime hours in the library. It's not hard to surmise what has caused your sudden inability to sleep here." He stopped pacing and faced me. "And I must implore you to stop meeting him at all ungodly hours of the night. I only agreed to come to Castle Combe if you were wise with your reputation, and it is clear you are not."

"James, we just talk. Nothing untoward has happened."

"That is beside the point. If I have heard you leave your room, doubtless others have as well. I will remind you this ill-begotten ruse is up in a few days and you will have to return to society. And I don't have to tell you how harsh they are. They do not care if you are just talking. You are alone with a man you are not betrothed to in the middle of the night."

"But what if this actually doesn't have to end in a few days? What if I don't need another season?"

James pinched the bridge of his nose, his other hand at his waist. "Oh my heavens, you have gone and fallen in love with him." It was very much not a question. I should have known James would see right through my continued insistence that all the time I spent with Andrew was to keep up appearances.

I didn't say anything, but apparently the expression on my face was all the answer James needed.

"Pack your things, we're leaving in the morning." James walked towards the bedroom door as if to signal that this conversation was over.

"No," I crossed my arms over my chest. "You and Charlotte can leave if you like, but I will stay until I've seen this through."

"I knew this was a terrible idea. I should have never agreed to this."

"Why is it so bad if I have fallen in love with him?"

"Because, Elinor, I told you. He does not intend to settle down. Whatever you hope will happen at the end of this house party, it won't go the way you think. He will break your heart."

"If my heart breaks, it will be *my* burden to bear." I leaned slightly toward him, pointing a finger at my own chest. "I'm not a child. You cannot protect me from every horrible thing in this life."

James let out a long sigh, walking over to sit at the edge of my bed and dropping his head into his hands. I don't know what it was about the gesture, but I was struck with a moment of clarity.

"James, you don't blame yourself, do you, for the heartache that Papa and Mama's deaths caused?" I sat on the bed next to him and placed a hand on his back.

When he looked at me again, his eyes were glassy with unshed tears. "You were still so young. You shouldn't have had to endure that."

"You shouldn't have had to either." I wrapped him in a hug. "And I would argue you bore more than I did because you stayed strong for me. You offered me security in all the uncertainty. You must know that you were the reason I made it through." I pulled back from our embrace, a hand on each shoulder as I held him at arm's length. "And if I am heart-broken at the end of this, you will be the reason I make it through that too."

"I hate to see you hurt."

"I know, but that is part of being human. We are the lucky ones, to know we can rely on each other in hard times. And good times, too."

James let out a long sigh. "You are far wiser than I am, Elinor. And you are right. No matter how much I wish to shield you, I cannot."

"I will be okay, I promise," I said, smiling. "For now, I think you should get some sleep and let tomorrow worry about its own problems."

CHAPTER 8

ANDREW

January 5, 1816

A day before the Twelfth Night ball, Father called me once again to his study. This time, he wasn't at his desk, but sitting in an armchair by the fire, reading. I shouldn't have been surprised that he didn't look up from his book when I entered, but it stung nonetheless. Would I, his only living son, ever be worth his attention?

"I am doubtful that your courtship and engagement to Lady Elinor is real," he said, turning a page, "but if it is, I insist that you break it."

"Elinor was the daughter of – and is now the sister of – an earl. Her dowry is more than sufficient, as are her accomplishments and talents. What possible objections can you have to a match like that?"

"Really, Andrew, proposing with a toad?" He snapped the book shut and stood. "That is further proof that you are not taking this seriously. And any young woman who accepts such a proposal is not fit to be your baroness."

I may not have ever been able to stand up for myself to my

father, but I couldn't – wouldn't – let him speak poorly of Elinor. I knew that if the roles were reversed and she was the one in front of my father, she would defend me. And I loved her even more for it.

"For my entire life, I have been trying to live up to Edward, to live up to your impossible and ever-changing standards. I know you don't understand me, but I'm happy. Elinor makes me happy. And nothing you say will change that."

I turned and stalked out of the study without being excused, knowing with absolute clarity what I had to do next.

I found Langley in the stables, preparing to take a morning ride.

"Morning, Fitz," he said, pulling on the saddle straps to make sure everything was securely fastened.

"I'd like to marry your sister."

He stopped what he was doing, but didn't turn to face me.

"You never told me I couldn't fall in love with her," I said, moving to stand on the other side of his horse so he was forced to look at me. "You only made me promise that her heart and her reputation would remain unscathed. And—" I stopped when I noticed James wasn't scowling or preparing to punch me square in the face. He was smiling.

"You love her?" he asked.

"With every part of my soul."

Langley let out a long sigh, and I could have been mistaken, but I thought I saw his eyes water. Perhaps it was the cold winter air, or the breeze that had just picked up.

"Are you crying?"

"No." Langley laughed, wiping at his eyes with the heel of his hand. "No, it's just that I am so relieved. Elinor told me of her feelings for you and I was prepared to hate you forever for breaking her heart."

"If you give me your blessing to marry her, I promise I will do everything in my power to make her happy every day of our lives. Her heart will always be safe with me."

"Of course you can marry her, Fitz. Everyone would have to be blind not to see how much she loves you and how happy you make her. And I could never forgive myself if I stood in the way of her happiness."

"Thank you," I reached over the horse, clapping a hand on Langley's shoulder. "Now if you'll excuse me, I must go in search of a toad."

"You cannot be serious," James chuckled, looking skyward. "What is Elinor going to do with a toad?"

"I don't know, but a boring old proposal just won't do. She deserves better than that," I called over my shoulder as I left the stables, feeling more alive than I had in my entire life.

CHAPTER 9

ELINOR

January 6, 1816

We would leave Castle Combe in the morning, and the time for telling Andrew my true feelings for him was running out. While I was certain he reciprocated my feelings, I wondered if my love – or his love for me – could outweigh his conviction not to marry.

I had hoped to find a private moment to talk with him during the afternoon before the Twelfth Night ball, but Andrew was outdoors with the rest of the men all day and I didn't see him before it was time to begin getting ready. I chose my favorite dress – a deep forest green one with ivory lace trimming on the neckline – and tried to clear my thoughts and calm my heart by focusing on my maid's hand as she swirled my hair into an intricate up-do.

As the ball began and the guests started filling the room, Andrew was still missing. What was taking him so long? The ball was at his family home, for heaven's sake, it's not like he had a long way to travel. My palms were sweaty and my long silk gloves only trapped the moisture to my skin, making me feel clammy.

Finally, I saw his tall figure enter the ballroom. He looked around, over the heads of all the guests. We locked eyes and I began walking toward him.

The room blurred around me as my heart picked up speed and I felt dizzy with the anticipation, but I gripped my reticule and forced one foot in front of the other until I was standing in front of Andrew. He stood with stiff posture, his hands behind his back. Perhaps this was going to be a terrible idea, but I was so close. All I had to do was open my mouth and begin the speech I had prepared and practiced over and over all afternoon.

"Elinor, I—" Andrew began.

"I know our agreement is meant to end tomorrow," I said, putting up a hand to cut him off. Despite how unladylike it was, I was desperate to get the words out before I lost my nerve. "And I also know how you feel about getting married. But I must ask you to reconsider. James strictly forbade me from falling in love with you, and I truly didn't mean to. But I have. And I am nearly certain you have fallen in love with me too." I stopped, reminding myself to take a deep, steadying breath before continuing.

He kept his hands behind his back, but his posture softened a bit and his mischievous grin gave me the courage to continue. "And if you gave us a chance, I promise I will love you for every day of my life. Whatever your father has told you all these years is wrong. You're not a disappointment, you will be the most wonderful Baron of Castle Combe. You are deserving of every wonderful thing life has to give you."

Without saying a word, he removed his hands from behind his back and lifted a toad toward me. I noticed a small bit of parchment had been tied around its broad throat with a red ribbon. In untidy scrawl, I saw the name Reginald written on the tag. I blinked a few times as my mind registered what he was handing me and what it meant. In the proposal story we made up on our first night in Castle Combe, Andrew proposed with a toad. I laughed until my stomach muscles ached and happy tears filled my eyes.

"Elinor Langley, the color of your eyes is at least one thousand times more beautiful than this toad, and I would love nothing more than to spend the rest of my life nailing down the perfect way to describe them."

Still laughing, I took Reginald from him, and lifted him up so I could look in his eyes. He was kind of cute, in a very ugly way.

"I didn't believe that I could love anyone the way I love you and I would count myself the luckiest man alive if you would be my wife. For real this time."

Still gripping my toad in one hand and stifling laughter, I flung my free arm around Andrew's neck and pulled his mouth to mine, hoping he could feel in my kiss how deeply I loved him, how perfect this proposal was. I pressed my forehead to his and closed my eyes.

"My heart beats for you, Andrew Fitzgerald. Marrying you will be the greatest adventure of my life."

Andrew laughed softly, leaving a trail of kisses from the tip of my nose all the way up to my hairline. "Second only to caring for a toad, I'm sure."

ABOUT THE AUTHOR

Madison Bailey read *Pride & Prejudice* for the first time when she was 14, and she hasn't put the romance novels down since. A Jane Austen fanatic and hopeful romantic, Madison writes clean and wholesome romances with guaranteed "Happily Ever Afters." When she's not writing, she loves reading, drinking hot chocolate, watching old Disney movies or reruns of The Office, and taking long naps and even longer bubble baths. She lives in Utah with her wonderful husband and their adorable puppy dog.

 instagram.com/author.madison.bailey

Milton Keynes UK
Ingram Content Group UK Ltd.
UKHW011950010124
435297UK00004B/258